# HOW TO DRAW MANGA

## with BEN DUNN

P9-BYY-439

2004 Antarctic Press

blished by Mud Puddle Books, Inc.
West 21st Street
ite 601
w York, New York 10010
o@mudpuddlebooks.com

BN: 1-59412-063-3

inted in the United States of America

KONNICHIWA! HA! BET YOU DIDN'T THINK I KNEW ANY JAPANESE DID YOU! ALL KIDDING ASIDE... I DON'T! WHAT I DO KNOW IS THAT I LOVE THE "MANGA" STYLE OF DRAWING! I SAY "MANGA" BECAUSE THERE ARE CERTAIN CHARACTERISTICS THAT SEPARATE IT FROM TRADITIONAL WESTERN COMICS. MORE ON THAT IN LATER CHAPTERS. WHAT I'LL COVER HERE ARE THE ELEMENTS OF MANGA THAT I HAVE CHOSEN TO USE IN MY OWN ART STYLE. I DO NOT PROFESS THIS TO BE THE ONLY WAY TO DO IT, BUT YOU WILL SEE THAT IT USES BASIC ELEMENTS THAT APPLY TO ALL STYLES. SO LET'S NOT WASTE ANY MORE TIME! LET'S ART MANGA!

## TOOLS OF THE TRADE!

BEFORE ONE CAN DRAW, ONE MUST HAVE THE RIGHT TOOLS. USE WHAT IS AVAILABLE! ADAPT WITH WHAT YOU KNOW. FOR ME, THE MOST COMMON TOOLS I DRAW WITH ARE: STAEDTLER PIGMENT LINERS (SIZES 01, 03, 05 AND 07), A ZEBRA 0.5 MECHANICAL PENCIL, TYPE HB LEAD, PARALLEL GLIDER RULER, LARGE RAISED-EDGE TRIANGLE, MARS MAGIC RUB ERASER, PEN BRUSH, OPAQUE BLACK INDIA INK, WHITE OUT, WHITE INK, OLD TOOTH-BRUSHES, RAISED-EDGE FRENCH CURVE, VARIOUS CIRCLE AND OVAL TEMPLATES, RAISED-EDGE RULER, FINE-POINT SHARPIE MARKERS, OLD RAGS, TWO LARGE JARS FILLED WITH WATER (ONE FOR CLEANING BLACK INK AND ONE FOR CLEANING WHITE INK), 15-INCH T-SQUARE AND 2-PLY, SMOOTH-SURFACE BRISTOL BOARD. GOT IT? GOOD, LET'S CONTINUE ON.

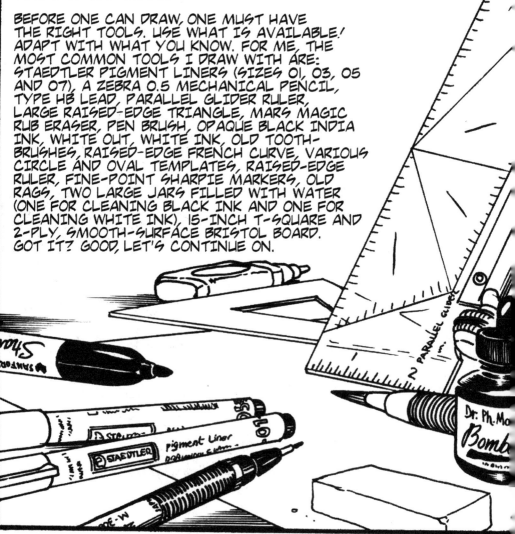

## BASIC BODY: THE MANNEQUIN

THE ENVIRONMENT

SURROUNDINGS ARE VERY IMPORTANT TO ME.
I PREFER AN AREA RELATIVELY CLEAN, A
SMOOTH DRAWING SURFACE WITH GOOD LIGHT,
AND A TAPE DECK TO POUND OUT SOME TUNES
DURING THOSE LATE-NIGHT DRAWING SHIFTS.
THIS IS WHAT WORKS FOR ME WHEN I AM IN
SERIOUS DRAWING MODE. YOU WILL FIND THAT
THE FEWER DISTRACTIONS YOU HAVE, THE MORE
YOU CAN CONCENTRATE
ON YOUR DRAWING!
HOWEVER, USE WHAT
YOU CAN AND ADAPT!
FOR YEARS I DREW ON
THE KITCHEN TABLE
OR ON THE FLOOR!

ATTITUDE!
THIS IS THE MOST IMPORTANT INGREDIENT!
IF YOU HAVE NO DESIRE TO DRAW OR IMPROVE,
THEN STOP RIGHT HERE! OTHERWISE, YOU MUST
NOT GIVE UP! PERFECTION ONLY COMES WITH
PRACTICE, PRACTICE, PRACTICE! EVEN I AM
STILL LEARNING NEW TRICKS!
YOUR LEVEL OF SKILL IS GOING TO BE, I ASSUME,
STILL AT THE BEGINNER'S STAGE. THINGS
LIKE PERSPECTIVE AND ANATOMY WILL COME
LATER IN THIS SERIES. IF YOU KNOW SOME OF
IT ALREADY, GREAT! IF NOT, DON'T WORRY,
WE WILL COVER THAT SOON ENOUGH!

# HOW TO DRAW MANGA

## BASIC BODY: THE MANNEQUIN

## BASIC BODY: THE MANNEQUIN

MY BASIC HUMAN STRUCTURE FOR THE AVERAGE NINJA HIGH SCHOOL CHARACTER BEGINS WITH WHAT I CALL THE "BALL AND SOCKET MANNEQUIN." ESSENTIALLY, THE BODY AND ITS JOINTS ARE SIMPLIFIED TO THE POINT WHERE THEY ARE SHOWN AS BALL AND SOCKETS.

HEAD AND SHOULDERS: THE HEAD IS CONNECTED AT THE BASE OF THE NECK SOCKET. YOU SHOULD TRY TO FOLLOW THE NATURAL MOVEMENT OF THE HEAD AS IT RELATES TO THE NECK AND SHOULDERS.

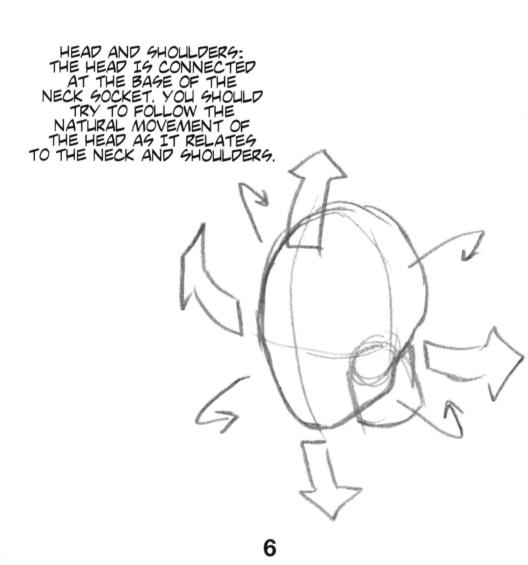

## BASIC BODY: THE MANNEQUIN

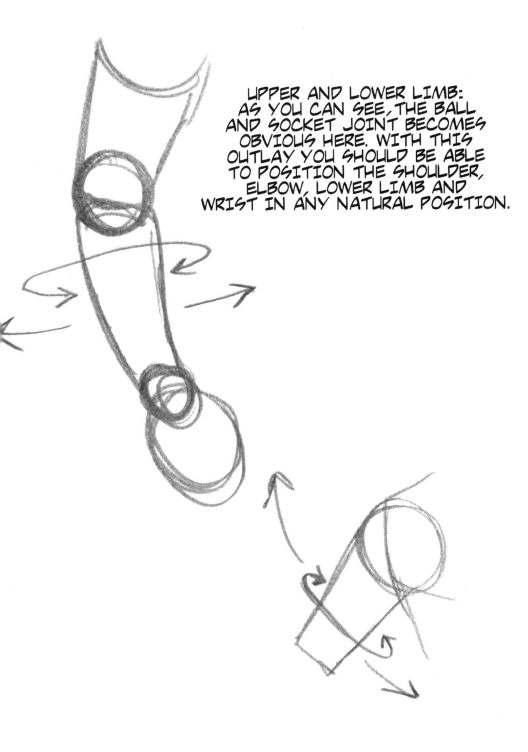

UPPER AND LOWER LIMB: AS YOU CAN SEE, THE BALL AND SOCKET JOINT BECOMES OBVIOUS HERE. WITH THIS OUTLAY YOU SHOULD BE ABLE TO POSITION THE SHOULDER, ELBOW, LOWER LIMB AND WRIST IN ANY NATURAL POSITION.

CHEST AND UPPER ABDOMEN:
AN OVAL BALL FITS NICELY BETWEEN THE UPPER RIB CAGE AND THE LOWER ABDOMEN. SLIDING IT AROUND, YOU CAN DRAW THE BODY IN NATURAL STANCES WITHOUT IT LOOKING AWKWARD.

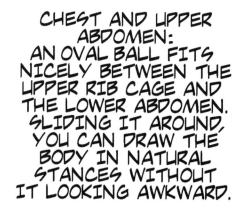

USE THE CENTER AXIS TO SHOW THE SPINE AND THEN DRAW THE BODY AROUND THAT SPINE!

8

# HOW TO DRAW MANGA

## BASIC BODY: THE MANNEQUIN

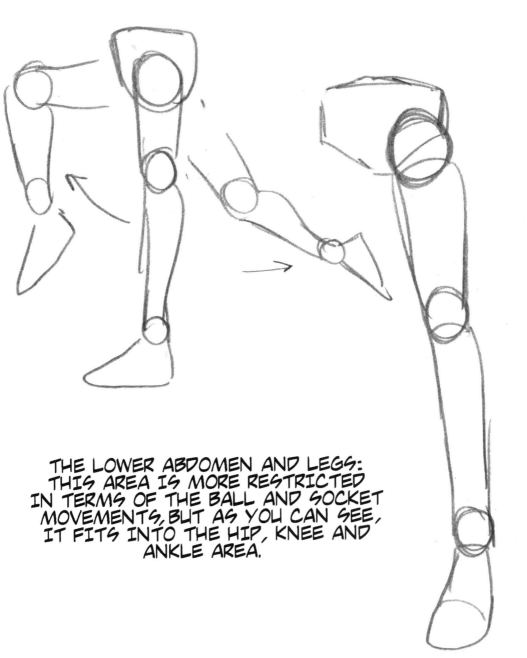

THE LOWER ABDOMEN AND LEGS:
THIS AREA IS MORE RESTRICTED
IN TERMS OF THE BALL AND SOCKET
MOVEMENTS, BUT AS YOU CAN SEE,
IT FITS INTO THE HIP, KNEE AND
ANKLE AREA.

## BASIC BODY: THE MANNEQUIN

DRAWING SECRET:
IF YOU REMEMBER THE BODY AS A SERIES OF INTERNAL PIPE BONES, YOU CAN PLAN THE STRUCTURE OF THE BODY EARLY AND THEN DRAW AROUND IT.

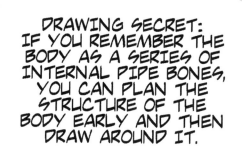

BY USING THE KNOWLEDGE OF PERSPECTIVE, YOU CAN USE THE MANNEQUIN AND PLACE YOUR CHARACTER IN MORE DRAMATIC AND EXCITING WAYS!

## BASIC BODY: THE MANNEQUIN

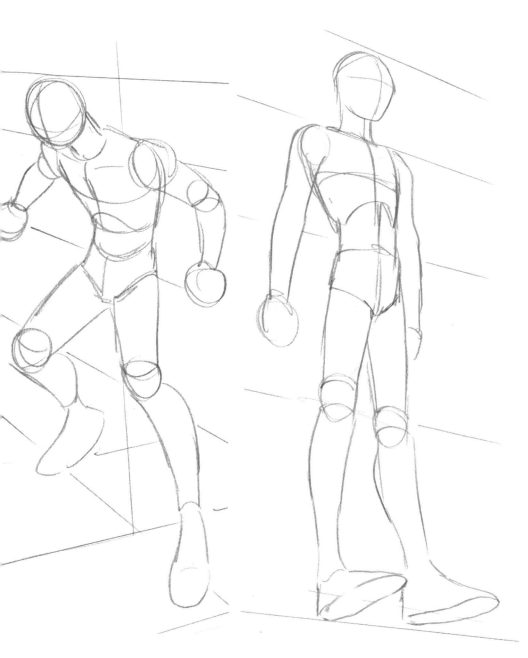

## BASIC BODY: THE MANNEQUIN

ONCE YOU'VE
MASTERED THE
MANNEQUIN FORM,
YOU CAN DRAW
YOUR CHARACTERS
IN ANY POSITION
IMAGINABLE!

# HOW TO DRAW MANGA

## BASIC BODY: THE MANNEQUIN

REMEMBER THE "THREE P'S": PRACTICE! PRACTICE! PRACTICE!

## BASIC BODY: THE MANNEQUIN

ALL RIGHT, THEN. NOW THAT WE'VE PRACTICED DRAWING FIGURES USING THE MANNEQUIN TECHNIQUE, LET US GET INTO WHAT IT TAKES TO DRAW A TYPICAL NINJA HIGH SCHOOL CHARACTER. FOR THE MOST PART, THE BASIC BODY STRUCTURE IS THE SAME FOR A MAJORITY OF NINJA HIGH SCHOOL CHARACTERS. THE THING THAT SEPARATES THEM IS THE WINDOW DRESSING. HOWEVER, LET ME REVIEW THE MALE AND FEMALE BODY STRUCTURES OF NHS.

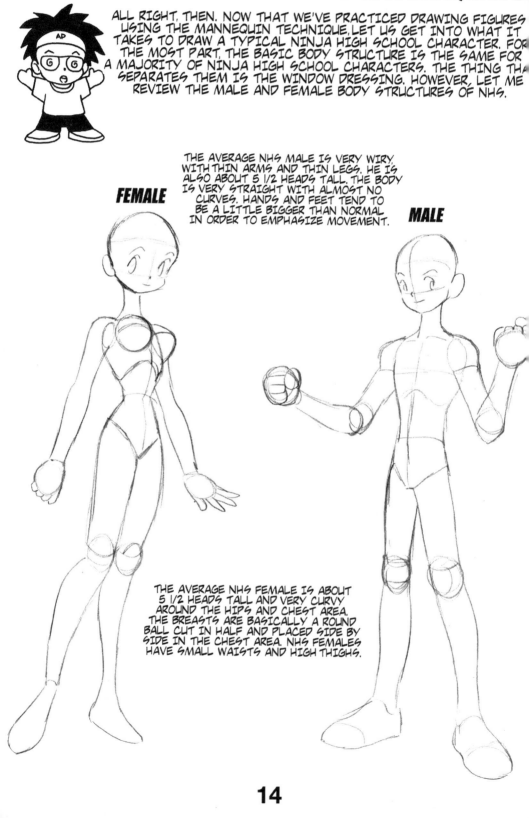

THE AVERAGE NHS MALE IS VERY WIRY, WITH THIN ARMS AND THIN LEGS. HE IS ALSO ABOUT 5 1/2 HEADS TALL. THE BODY IS VERY STRAIGHT WITH ALMOST NO CURVES. HANDS AND FEET TEND TO BE A LITTLE BIGGER THAN NORMAL IN ORDER TO EMPHASIZE MOVEMENT.

**FEMALE**

**MALE**

THE AVERAGE NHS FEMALE IS ABOUT 5 1/2 HEADS TALL AND VERY CURVY AROUND THE HIPS AND CHEST AREA. THE BREASTS ARE BASICALLY A ROUND BALL CUT IN HALF AND PLACED SIDE BY SIDE IN THE CHEST AREA. NHS FEMALES HAVE SMALL WAISTS AND HIGH THIGHS.

# HOW TO DRAW MANGA

## DRAWING THE HEAD

NOW WE BEGIN TO CONSTRUCT THE FIGURE. I USUALLY START WITH THE HEAD BEFORE I DO THE REST OF THE BODY. LET'S PRACTICE A LITTLE WITH THE HEAD, SHALL WE?

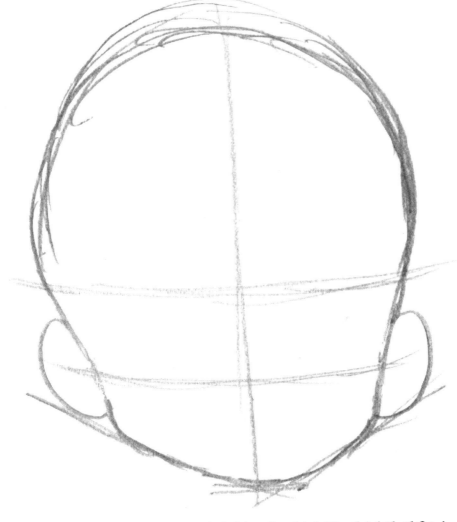

START A CIRCLE AND SKETCH A LOWER JAW AROUND IT. PENCIL IN THE EYE AREA, NOSE AREA, AND MOUTH AREA.

## DRAWING THE HEAD

# STEP TWO

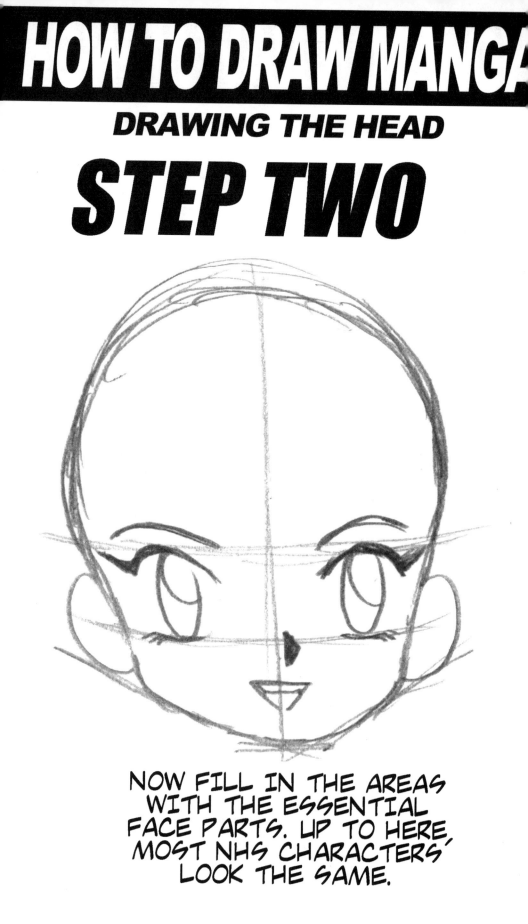

NOW FILL IN THE AREAS
WITH THE ESSENTIAL
FACE PARTS. UP TO HERE,
MOST NHS CHARACTERS'
LOOK THE SAME.

## DRAWING THE HEAD

# STEP THREE

NOW HERE IS WHERE WE ADD THE DETAILS. I'VE ADDED A HAIRLINE SO I KNOW WHERE THE HAIR WILL FALL.

# HOW TO DRAW MANGA

## DRAWING THE HEAD

# STEP FOUR

THEN I INK THE APPROPRIATE LINES
AND ERASE THE PENCIL LINES. NOW
WE HAVE THE FINISHED PRODUCT.

## DRAWING THE HEAD

NOW LET'S TRY THE HEAD AT A
SLIGHTLY DIFFERENT ANGLE.

START WITH A CIRCLE AND
WORK IN THE BASIC FACE
STRUCTURE.

19

## DRAWING THE HEAD

# STEP TWO

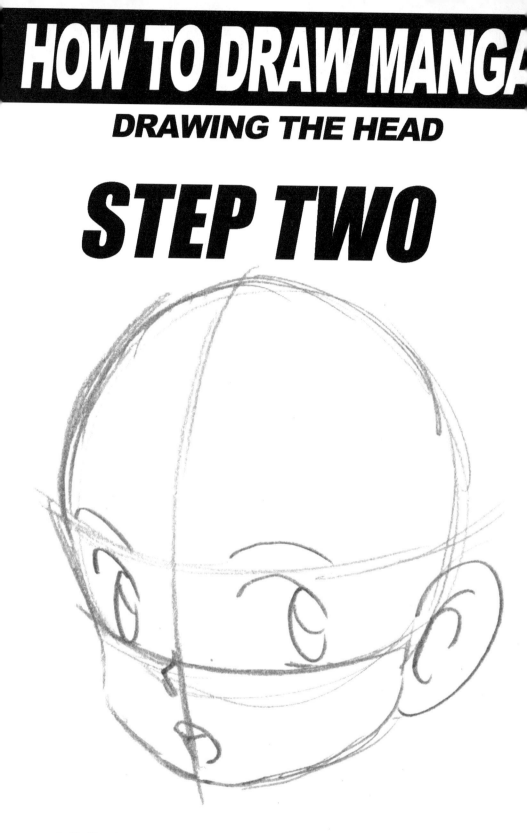

ADD IN EYES, NOSE AND MOUTH.

# STEP THREE

ADD HAIRLINE AND
BEGIN TO ADD DETAILS
TO THE FACE TO MAKE IT
UNIQUE.

# HOW TO DRAW MANGA

## DRAWING THE HEAD

# STEP FOUR

ERASE THE PENCILS,
AND VOILA! YOU'RE
DOING GREAT!

## DRAWING THE HEAD

THE HEAD IS PERHAPS THE MOST IMPORTANT PART OF THE BODY IN TERMS OF ARTISTIC EXPRESSION. IT IS THIS PART THAT MOST PEOPLE SEE EVERYDAY, AND IN MANGA THE HEAD SAYS EVERYTHING ABOUT THE CHARACTER! TRY DESIGNING YOUR OWN CHARACTERS STARTING WITH THE HEAD AND SEE WHAT YOU COME UP WITH!

## DRAWING THE HEAD

## LET'S DRAW A FIGURE!

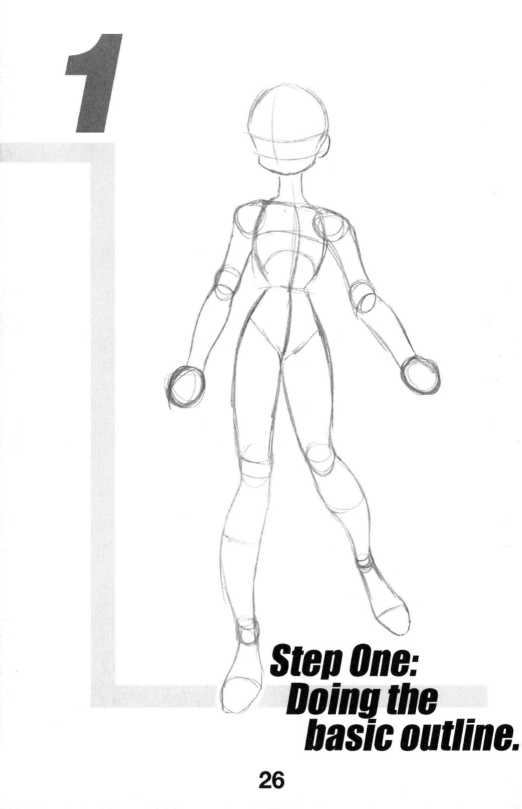

**1**

## Step One: Doing the basic outline.

# HOW TO DRAW MANGA

## LET'S DRAW A FIGURE!

**2**

## Step Two: Adding in the details.

# HOW TO DRAW MANGA

## LET'S DRAW A FIGURE!

**Step Three: Inking and rendering the figure.**

# HOW TO DRAW MANGA
## LET'S DRAW A FIGURE!

**4**

**Step Four:
Final inking
and erasing.**

## BODY LANGUAGE

THE HUMAN BODY IS THE MOST IMPORTANT FACTOR IN DOING A STORY (UNLESS IT'S NOT ABOUT PEOPLE, IN WHICH CASE THIS IS MOOT)! SO IT IS IMPORTANT TO UNDERSTAND WHAT A CHARACTER MEANS IN ORDER TO ADVANCE THE STORY, TELEGRAPH AN ACTION, OR DEFINE THE CHARACTER!

FISTS CLENCHED TO SHOW POWER

EYES FOCUSED FOWARD

FINGER EMPHASIS IMPORTANT

MOUTH OPEN TO INDICATE SPEAKING

LEGS SPREAD APART TO SHOW RIGIDITY

SINCE WE ARE MELDING STORY NARRATIVE WITH GRAPHIC INTERPRETATION, IT IS NECESSARY TO UNDERSTAND THE FUNDAMENTALS OF BODY LANGUAGE!

THE BODY CAN SAY MANY THINGS IN MANGA. IT CAN TELL THE READER THE PERSONALITY, MOOD, DISPOSITION, AND EMOTIONAL STATE OF THE CHARACTER! WHAT THE CHARACTER DOESN'T SAY CAN BE JUST AS IMPORTANT AS WHAT THE CHARACTER DOES SAY! NOW, BEFORE WE BEGIN, LET ME SHOW YOU MY APPROACH TO THE DIFFERENT GENDERS.

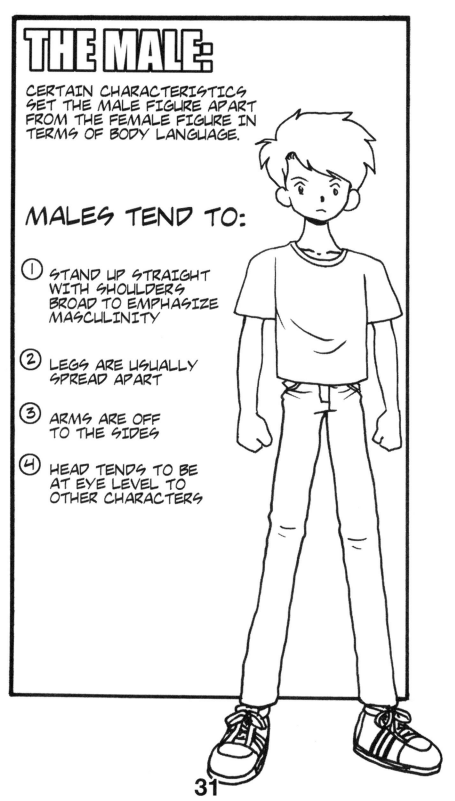

## THE MALE:

CERTAIN CHARACTERISTICS SET THE MALE FIGURE APART FROM THE FEMALE FIGURE IN TERMS OF BODY LANGUAGE.

## MALES TEND TO:

1. STAND UP STRAIGHT WITH SHOULDERS BROAD TO EMPHASIZE MASCULINITY

2. LEGS ARE USUALLY SPREAD APART

3. ARMS ARE OFF TO THE SIDES

4. HEAD TENDS TO BE AT EYE LEVEL TO OTHER CHARACTERS

## BODY LANGUAGE

# THE FEMALE:

THE CHARACTERISTICS OF THIS GENDER ARE THAT THEY ARE SOFT AND CURVY.

## FEMALES TEND TO:

1 SHOULDERS TEND TO BE A LITTLE MORE RELAXED

2 THE FIGURE TENDS TO CURVE OFF CENTER

3 ARMS ARE CLOSER TO THE BODY

4 LEGS ARE USUALLY CLOSER TOGETHER

# HOW TO DRAW MANGA

## BODY LANGUAGE
### THE RELAXED FIGURE

BODIES AT REST TEND TO STAY AT REST. WHEN DRAWING THE FIGURE AT REST, DON'T SHOW A STIFF AND UNNATURAL FIGURE, BUT SHOW A FIGURE REALLY AT REST! EVEN AT REST, THE FIGURE CAN BE SHOWN DRAMATICALLY!

## BODY LANGUAGE
### THE RELAXED FIGURE

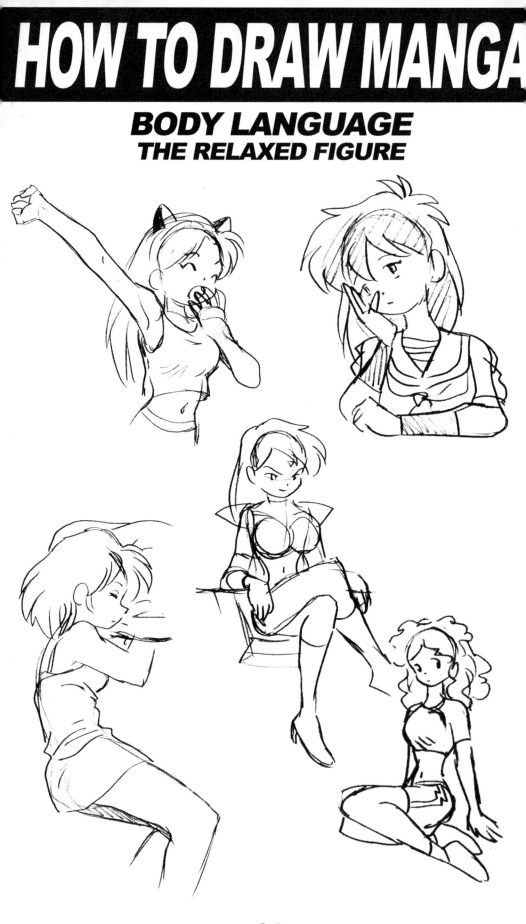

## BODY LANGUAGE
### THE BODY IN MOTION

SHOWING THE BODY IN DRAMATIC POSES IS WHAT MANGA IS ALL ABOUT. ONE TRICK TO REMEMBER IS THE "SPINE AND MANNEQUIN" TECHNIQUE. WITH THIS, YOU CAN DRAW THE BODY IN ALMOST ANY POSITION.

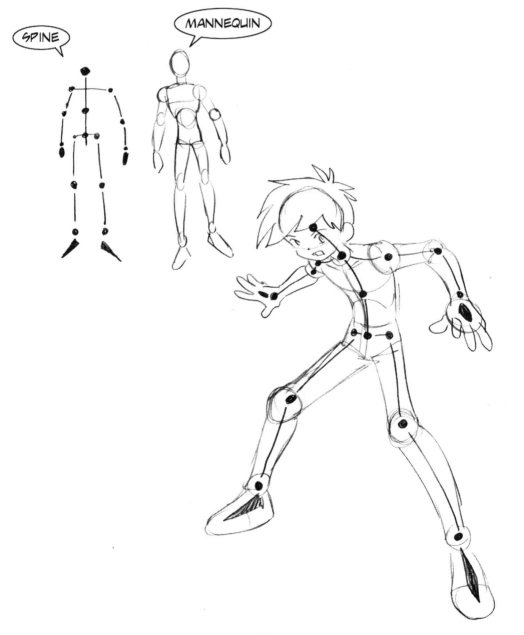

## BODY LANGUAGE
### THE BODY IN MOTION

THE EMPHASIS IS ON MOTION! WHEN SHOWING CHARACTERS IN MOTION, MAKE IT MEAN SOMETHING! DEFINE AND DEFY!

ATTACK!

ESTABLISH MOTION FLOW AND LET THE BODY FOLLOW IT!

DEFENSE

**36**

## BODY LANGUAGE
### FIGHT SCENES

N MANGA, BODIES CAN DO ANYTHING! YOU ARE NOT LIMITED BY TIME, SPACE, OR GRAVITY! IT IS ALWAYS BEST TO "FOLLOW THE FLOW" IN ORDER TO ACHIEVE SOME BELIEVABILITY. FOR EXAMPLE:

ICHI DECIDES TO DO A STANDARD RUNNING ATTACK!

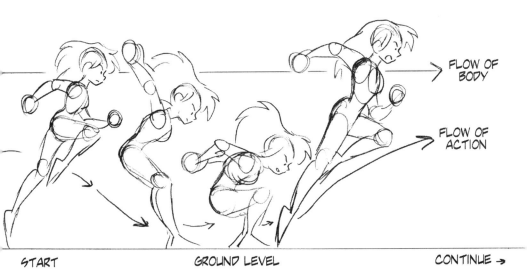

**37**

## BODY LANGUAGE
### FIGHT SCENES

CONTINUE →

VICTIM →

FINISH

OF COURSE ASRIAL WOULDN'T SIMPLY LET ICHI ATTACK HER, SO SHE WILL DEFEND IN A WAY THAT WOULD COUNTER ICHI'S FLYING ATTACK!

## BODY LANGUAGE
### FIGHT SCENES

THERE ARE MANY WAYS THAT ASRIAL COULD COUNTER ICHI'S ATTACK!

SHE COULD DUCK! THIS DEFENSE IS MORE SUBMISSIVE AND IS USUALLY USED MORE TO JUST GET OUT OF THE WAY!

SHE COULD DODGE! THIS IS MORE REACTIVE AND INDICATES SHE IS WILLING TO PROLONG THE CONFLICT!

THERE ARE OTHER OPTIONS DEPENDING ON HOW YOU WANT TO ADVANCE THE STORY.

SHE COULD BLOCK!

OR SHE COULD GRAB ICHI ROUGHLY ABOUT THE SHOULDERS AND DRAW HER CLOSE TO HER LIPS AND...

SHE COULD LEAP OR JUMP!

SHE COULD PULL A WEAPON OUT OF NOWHERE AND COUNTER-ATTACK!

COOL OFF!

BOOM!

HEY! BEN! GET BACK ON THE SUBJECT!! THIS ISN'T "NOT NINJA HIGH SCHOOL," YOU KNOW!

39

## BODY LANGUAGE
### FIGHT SCENES

*AHEM*... YES. WELL, YOU GET THE IDEA. THE NAME OF THE GAME IS MOVEMENT, OR AT LEAST THE IDEA OF MOVEMENT. SINCE MANGA IS A STATIC, TWO-DIMENSION MEDIUM, YOU HAVE TO GIVE THE READER THE IDEA THAT YOUR CHARACTERS ARE MOVING WHEN THEY ARE NOT. SINCE NHS IS A HUMOR BOOK, THE FIGHT SCENES TEND TO BE MORE OUTRAGEOUS. HERE ARE SOME STANDARD STOCK FIGHT SCENES I TEND TO EMPLOY. ALLOW ICHI TO DEMONSTRATE AS LENDO VOLUNTEERS.

STAR FOR EFFECT

THE "ONE FOOT IN THE FACE"

# HOW TO DRAW MANGA

## BODY LANGUAGE
### FIGHT SCENES

THE "TWO FEET IN THE FACE" JUMP ATTACK

## BODY LANGUAGE
### FIGHT SCENES

THE BACK
FLIP

ALL
RIGHT!
I GIVE
UP!!

# HOW TO DRAW MANGA

## BODY LANGUAGE
### FIGHT SCENES

OF COURSE, NOT EVERYONE IS AS EASY AS LENDO. A TYPICAL FIGHT SCENE
CONTAINS THE FOUR "C"S.

① CONFRONTATION

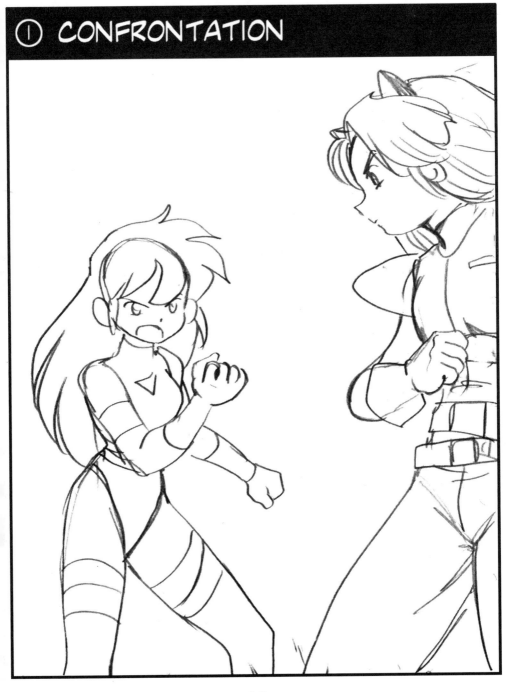

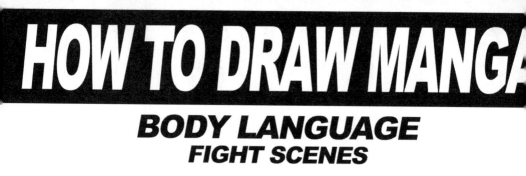

# HOW TO DRAW MANGA

## BODY LANGUAGE
### FIGHT SCENES

② CONFLICT

## BODY LANGUAGE
### FIGHT SCENES

③ CLIMAX

## BODY LANGUAGE
### FIGHT SCENES

④ CONCLUSION

## BODY LANGUAGE

ERE ARE SOME OTHER ACTIONS THAT YOU MIGHT FIND USEFUL.

## BODY LANGUAGE

## BODY LANGUAGE
### FIGHT SCENES

THE FACE IS THE FOCUS OF ATTENTION ON THE HUMAN BODY. IT CAN SAY SO MUCH WITHOUT SAYING ANYTHING AT ALL. HERE ARE SOME STANDARD EXPRESSIONS I USE IN NHS...

VERY HAPPY OR
EXCITED

HAPPY OR
PLEASED

WILY

CACKLING

**49**

## BODY LANGUAGE
### EXPRESSIONS

APOLOGETIC

ANGRY
SHOUTING

SAD

SURPRISE OR
SHOCK

## BODY LANGUAGE
### EXPRESSIONS

ANGRY
GRITTING

MODEST

BORED

SNOTTY

YOU CAN MIX AND MATCH EMOTIONS TO CONVEY A CERTAIN
LOOK TO EACH CHARACTER.

BEFORE I WAS EXPOSED TO MANGA, I WAS AN AVID SUPERHERO COMIC READER (ESPECIALLY MARVEL)! IN FACT, WHEN I WAS A KID, I WANTED TO WORK FOR MARVEL, SO I SENT IN A SUBMISSION! IT WAS REJECTED, BUT I GOT A COOL LETTER FROM ONE OF THE EDITORS SAYING WHY I WASN'T GOOD ENOUGH! BUT I WASN'T DISCOURAGED!

THEN, IN 1977, I WENT TO TAIWAN AND WAS EXPOSED TO MANGA! I KNEW THIS WAS MY CALLING! MANGA SHOWED ME A NEW DIRECTION IN COMICS THAT WOULD FOREVER CHANGE MY PERCEPTION OF ITS TRUE POTENTIAL! FROM THERE ON, I VOWED TO SHOW EVERYONE THE WORLD OF MANGA!

BUT I STILL LOVED SUPERHERO COMICS! I WAS CONFUSED UNTIL I MET MY JAPANESE PEN-PAL AKIHIRO! HE WAS THE GUY IN CHARGE OF THE C.L.A. (COMICS LOVERS ASSOCIATION). HIS CLUB PUT OUT A FANZINE CALLED "JUSTICE" THAT SHOWED ME A MIX OF MANGA ART WITH WESTERN-STYLE SUPERHEROES, OUT OF WHICH CAME A SYNTHESIS THAT I HAD NEVER SEEN BEFORE...

ANATOMY IS IMPORTANT IN DRAWING REALISTIC CHARACTERS. THIS APPLIES TO MANGA AS WELL AS TO SUPERHERO COMICS. KNOWING WHERE THE MUSCLE GROUPS GO WILL HELP IN MAKING THE CHARACTERS MORE BELIEVABLE AND IN KEEPING THEM CONSISTENT. DYNAMIC ANATOMY IS THE ART OF TAKING THE HUMAN BODY AND POSING IT SO THAT IT SHOWS MOVEMENT AND ACTION! WHEN I DRAW HEROIC CHARACTERS, I OFTEN OVERDO THE LINES AND SHOW MUSCLES THAT REALLY DO NOT EXIST BUT GIVE THE CHARACTER MORE DYNAMISM! IT IS IMPORTANT TO KNOW WHERE EVERYTHING IS, BUT YOU DON'T ALWAYS HAVE TO DRAW EVERY MUSCLE, AND BY THE SAME TOKEN, YOU CAN SOMETIMES OVEREXAGGERATE. THE KEY IS TO HAVE FUN WHILE KEEPING WITHIN THE PARAMETERS OF REALISTIC ANATOMY.

# HOW TO DRAW MANGA

## ANATOMY
### THE NECK

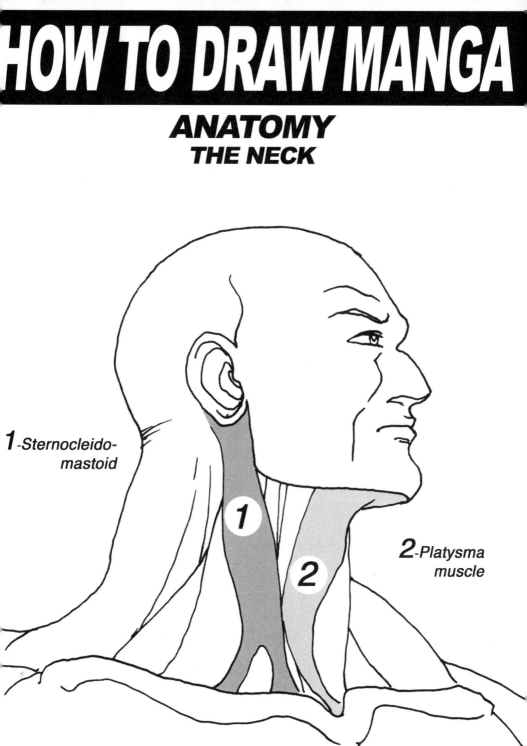

1-Sternocleido-
mastoid

2-Platysma
muscle

## ANATOMY
### THE NECK

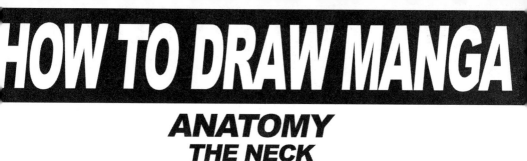

# HOW TO DRAW MANGA

## ANATOMY
### THE NECK

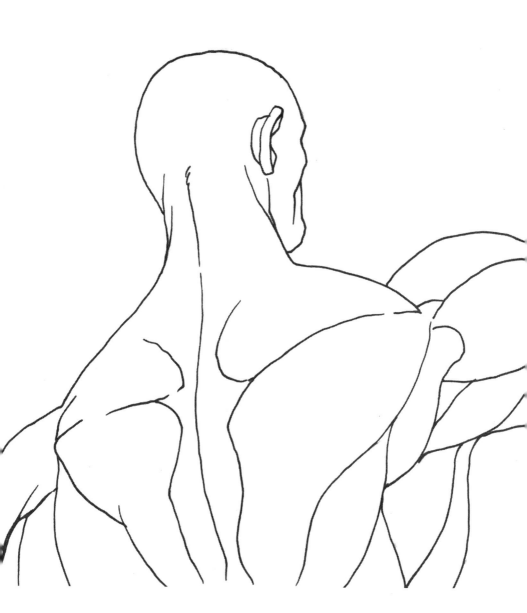

## ANATOMY
### THE NECK

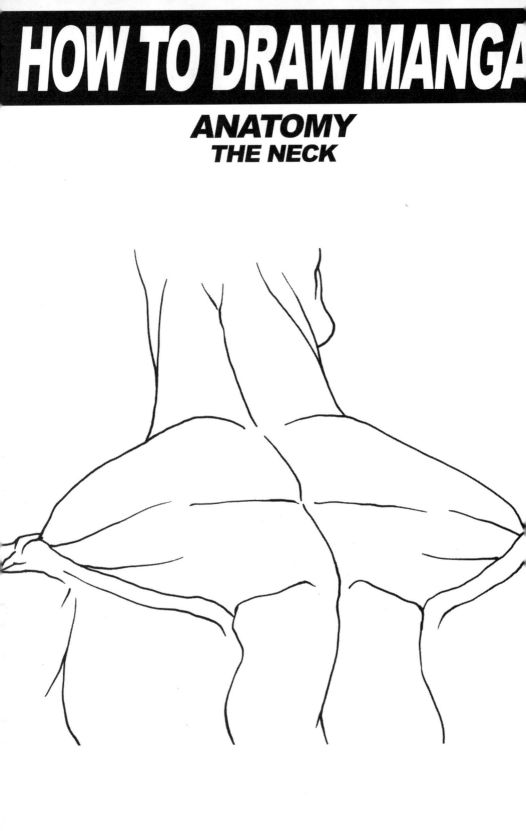

# HOW TO DRAW MANGA

## ANATOMY
### THE BACK

*1*-Trapezius

*2*-Latissimus

*3*-External oblique

*4*-Gluteus maximus

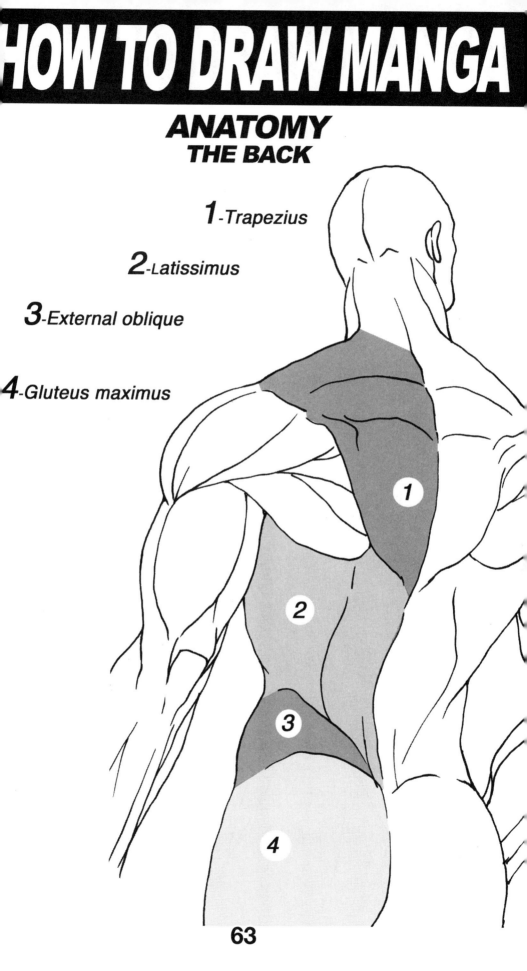

## ANATOMY
### THE FRONT

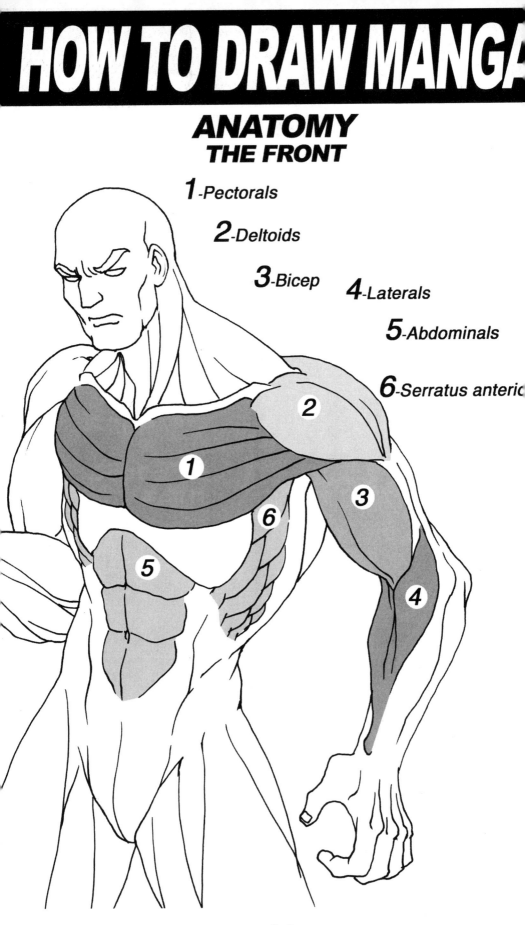

**1**-Pectorals

**2**-Deltoids

**3**-Bicep

**4**-Laterals

**5**-Abdominals

**6**-Serratus anteric

## ANATOMY
### THE ARM

**1**-Deltoid

**2**-Bicep

**3**-Brachio radialis

**4**-Superficial anterior forearm

**a**-Tricep

**b**-Elbow

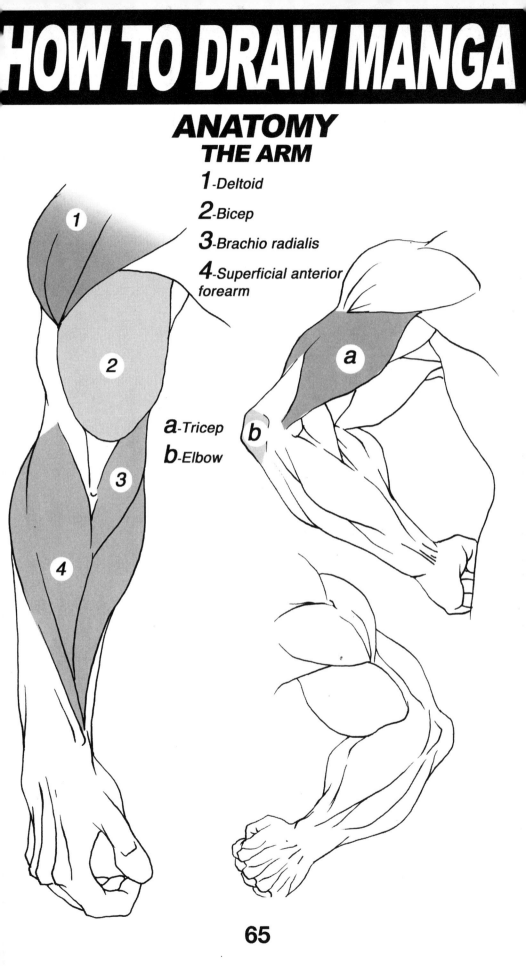

## BODY TYPES
### MALE BODY TYPE

SUPERHEROES AND VILLAINS HAVE SEVERAL BODY TYPES. THE TYPE OF BODY ONE CHOOSES SAYS A GREAT DEAL ABOUT THE CHARACTER.

### BODYBUILDER TYPE (AVERAGE)

A TYPICAL SUPERHERO OR VILLAIN BODY TYPE.

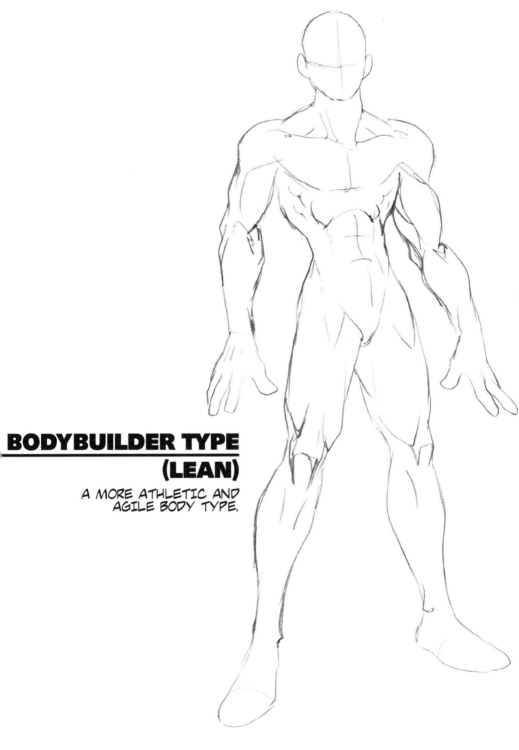

## BODYBUILDER TYPE (LEAN)

A MORE ATHLETIC AND AGILE BODY TYPE.

## BODY TYPES

### BODYBUILDER TYPE

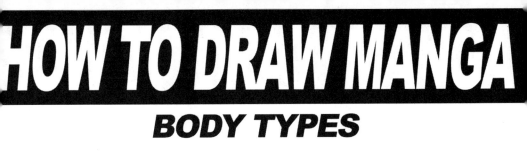

# HOW TO DRAW MANGA

## BODY TYPES

**SKINNY TEEN TYPE**

NOTE:
THE THINNER THE NECK,
THE THINNER THE BODY.

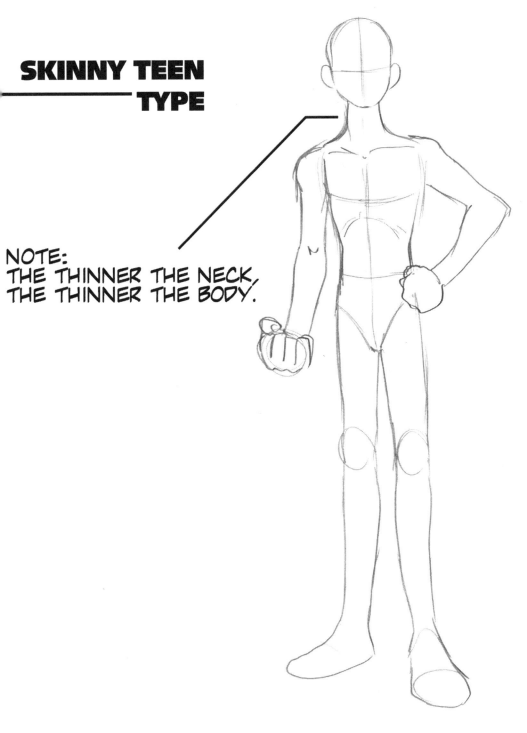

## BODY TYPES

NOTE:
A SMALLER HEAD INDICATES
MORE BODY MASS

## CHUNKY TYPE

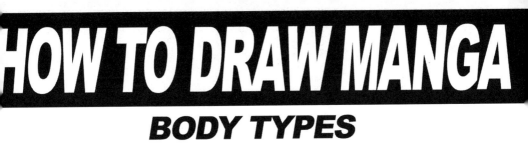

# HOW TO DRAW MANGA
## BODY TYPES

### PRE-TEEN BOY

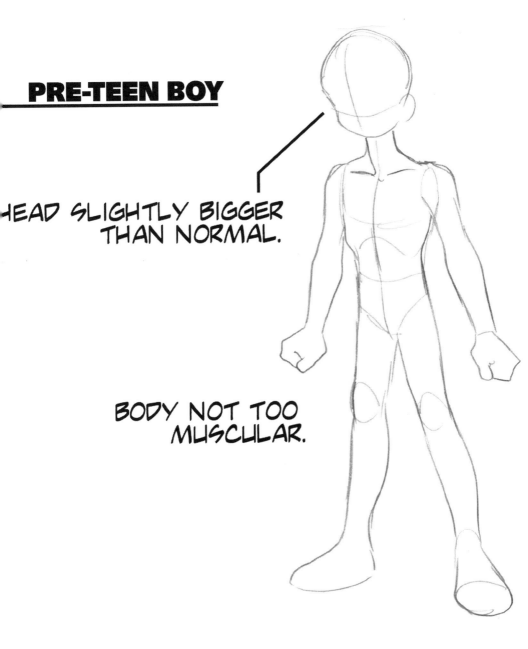

HEAD SLIGHTLY BIGGER THAN NORMAL.

BODY NOT TOO MUSCULAR.

# HOW TO DRAW MANGA

## BODY TYPES
### THE HUSKY, MUSCULAR MALE HERO/VILLAIN

## BODY TYPES

## BODY TYPES
## FEMALE BODY TYPE

FEMALES TEND TO BE LESS MUSCULAR AND MORE CURVEY TO HEIGHTEN THEIR FEMININITY.

## AMAZON TYPE

## BODY TYPES

### AVERAGE TYPE

## BODY TYPES

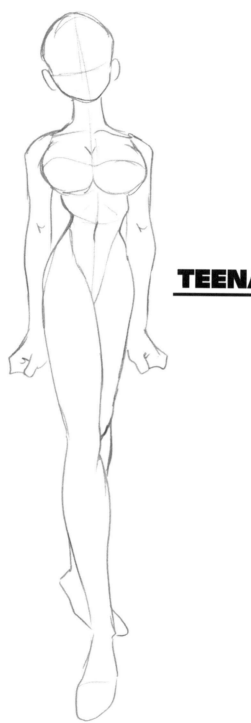

### TEENAGE GIRL TYPE

## BODY TYPES

## PRE-TEEN GIRL TYPE

## BODY TYPES

THE **HEROIC FEMALE**

OR **EVIL VILLAINESS**

## CAPES!

CAPE SHOULD
FLOW OVER THE
BODY OF THE
CHARACTER.

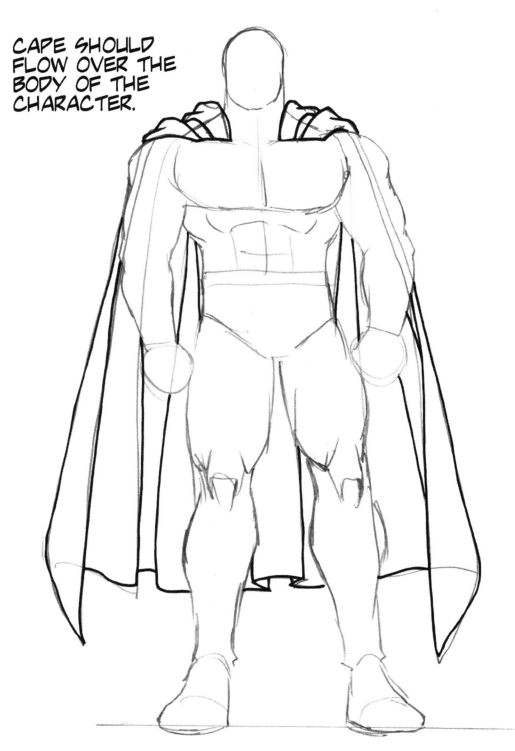

## CAPES!

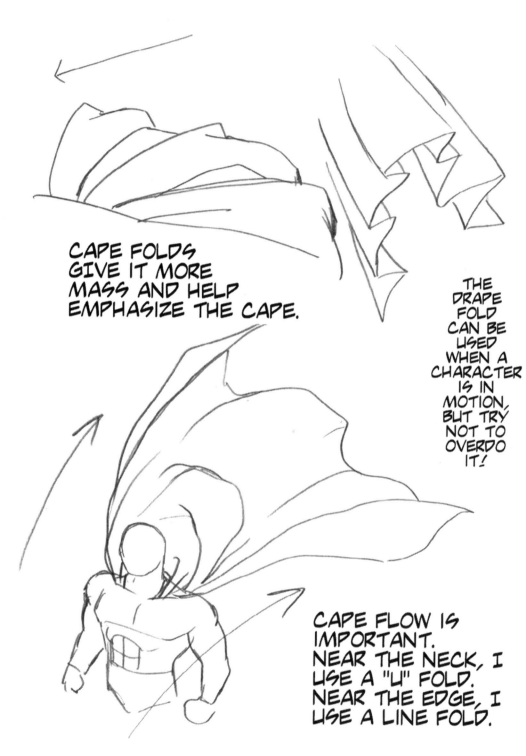

CAPE FOLDS
GIVE IT MORE
MASS AND HELP
EMPHASIZE THE CAPE.

THE
DRAPE
FOLD
CAN BE
USED
WHEN A
CHARACTER
IS IN
MOTION,
BUT TRY
NOT TO
OVERDO
IT!

CAPE FLOW IS
IMPORTANT.
NEAR THE NECK, I
USE A "U" FOLD.
NEAR THE EDGE, I
USE A LINE FOLD.

## CAPES!

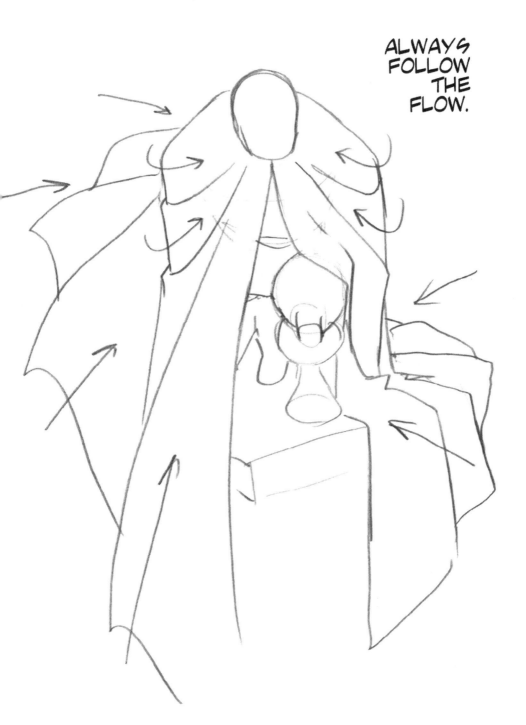

ALWAYS
FOLLOW
THE
FLOW.

## CAPES!

FOLDS ARE VERY
IMPORTANT FOR GIVING
THE CAPE MOVEMENT
AND DRAMA.

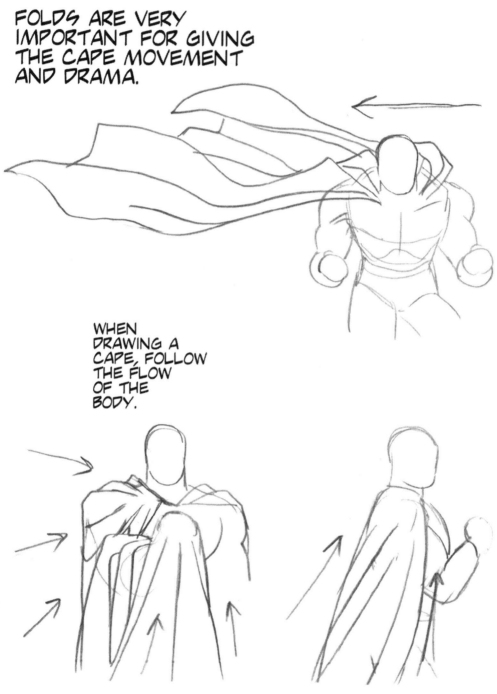

WHEN
DRAWING A
CAPE, FOLLOW
THE FLOW
OF THE
BODY.

## CAPES!

EVEN THOUGH CAPES MAY NOT FLOW LIKE THIS IN REAL LIFE, I LIKE TO OVER-DRAMATIZE THE MOVEMENT TO GIVE IT IMPACT!

WHEN DRAWING CAPES FLAPPING IN THE WIND, I TRY NOT TO DRAW JUST A STRAIGHT LINE. I LIKE TO SHOW "WAVES" TO MAKE THE CAPE LOOK LIKE IT'S MOVING.

## CAPES!

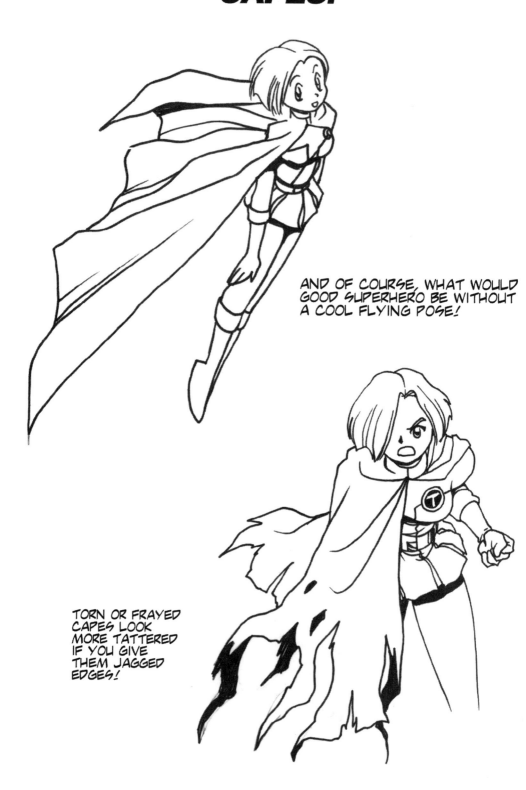

AND OF COURSE, WHAT WOULD GOOD SUPERHERO BE WITHOUT A COOL FLYING POSE!

TORN OR FRAYED CAPES LOOK MORE TATTERED IF YOU GIVE THEM JAGGED EDGES!

# HOW TO DRAW MANGA

## DRAW ICHI KUN

ONE OF THE MORE POPULAR CHARACTERS IN NINJA HIGH SCHOOL IS THE NINJA FEMME FATALE, ICHI KUN ICHINOHEI. ORIGINALLY CALLED ITCHY KOO, SHE HAS PROVEN TO BE ONE OF THE MORE INTERESTING CHARACTERS TO DRAW.

IF YOU HAVE SOME OF THE EARLIER EDITIONS OF HOW TO DRAW MANGA, YOU'VE LEARNED THE BASIC BODY TYPES AND HOW TO CONSTRUCT THEM.

ICHI CAN BE CLASSIFIED AS AN "AVERAGE FEMALE ANIME TYPE" BODY. THE MAIN THING IS THE SAILOR SUIT SHE WEARS. THAT IS HER TRADEMARK.

87

## DRAW ICHI KUN

ICHI'S NINJA OUTFIT IS NOT THE TRADITIONAL LOOSE GARB OF A NINJA, BUT A SKINTIGHT NUMBER WITH FLOWING SASHES. NOT EXACTLY REGULATION NINJA CLOTHING, BUT THEN, SHE ISN'T AN ORDINARY NINJA.

ICHI'S SISTER, HITOMI, WEARS A LONG SKIRT, DARK NAVY BLUE IN COLOR, FOR A UNIFORM. THIS IS ACTUALLY MORE IN LINE WITH WHAT REAL JAPANESE SCHOOLGIRLS WEAR.

ICHI'S SKIRT COMES DOWN TO HER KNEES AND IS PLEATED. THE BEST WAY TO DRAW THE PLEATS IS TO FOLLOW THE FLOW OF THE DRESS.

THE SHIRT IS A PULLOVER WITH NO BUTTONS.

## DRAW ICHI KUN

WHEN DRAWING THE SKIRT IN MOTION, FOLLOW THE DIRECTION OF THE MOVEMENT OR THE WIND.

## DRAW ICHI KUN

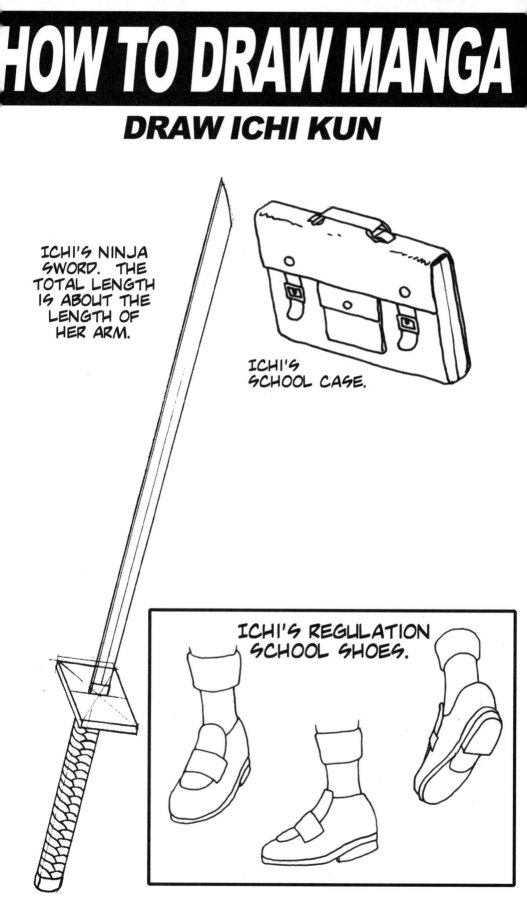

ICHI'S NINJA
SWORD. THE
TOTAL LENGTH
IS ABOUT THE
LENGTH OF
HER ARM.

ICHI'S
SCHOOL CASE.

ICHI'S REGULATION
SCHOOL SHOES.

**1**

2

## DRAW ICHI KUN

## DRAW ICHI KUN

# HOW TO DRAW MANGA

## DRAW ICHI KUN

# HOW TO DRAW MANGA

## DRAW ICHI KUN

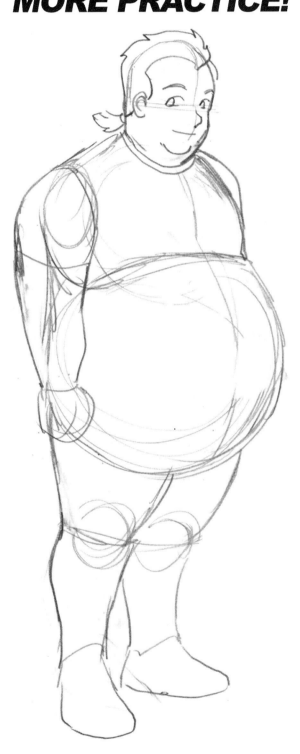

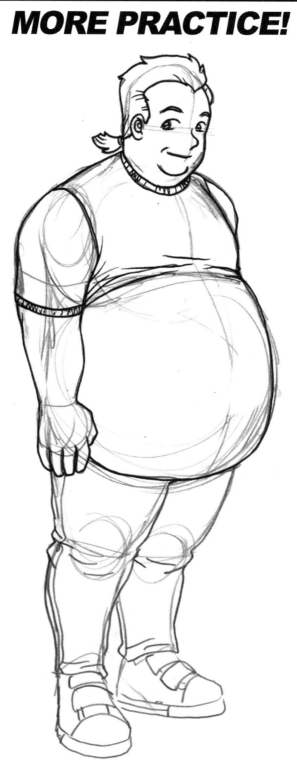

# HOW TO DRAW MANGA
## MORE PRACTICE!

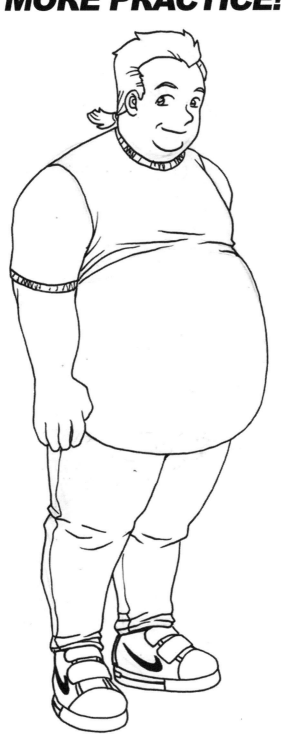

# HOW TO DRAW MANGA

## DRAW A KAT-GIRL

ONE OF THE MOST ENDURING MANGA-TYPE CHARACTERS IS KNOWN AS THE "NEKO" OR "CAT-GIRL". THEY ARE USUALLY VERY CUTE AND SPIRITED TYPES OF CHARACTERS AND ADD A SENSE OF QUIRKINESS TO ANY MANGA STORY.

THERE ARE CERTAINLY MANY TYPES OF FURRY GIRLS, BUT CATS SEEM TO FIT FEMALES THE BEST, SINCE FEMALES TEND TO BE CATLIKE IN MANGA. I WON'T SAY THIS IS THE ONLY WAY TO DO THIS, BUT I THINK THESE ARE THE BASICS TO START YOUR OWN CAT-GIRL CHARACTER! MEOW! MEOW!

# HOW TO DRAW MANGA

## DRAW A KAT-GIRL
### BODY TYPES

### 1. HUMAN/CAT-GIRL HYBRID

This is basically a human body with cat ears. Simple and direct. Not too catlike.

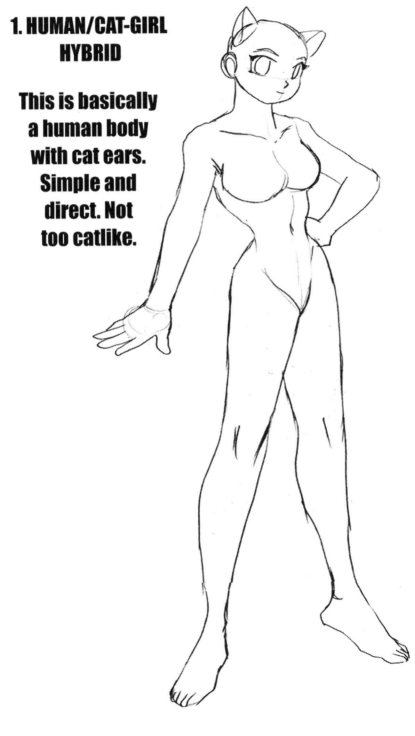

## DRAW A KAT-GIRL
### BODY TYPES

**2. CAT-GIRL
AVERAGE BUILD**

More "catty." Big
eyes with cat pupils
or human pupils (if
that is you choice).
Hands are more
"pawlike." Add
tail to complete
the body.

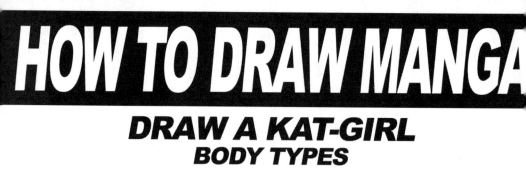

## DRAW A KAT-GIRL
### BODY TYPES

### 3. CAT-GIRL MUSCULAR BUILD

This version of the cat-girl is larger and more heroric in proportions. Good for use in superhero stories. I draw CHEETAH from GOLD DIGGER this way.

## DRAW A KAT-GIRL
### BODY TYPES

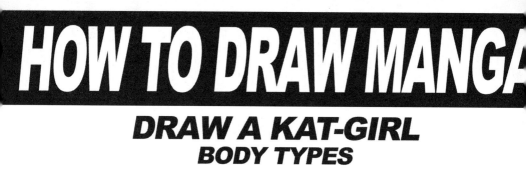

**4. CAT-GIRL
SPEEDY BUILD**

**This version of
the cat-girl is
thin and has
a runner's
build. Makes
for more
stealthy
look.**

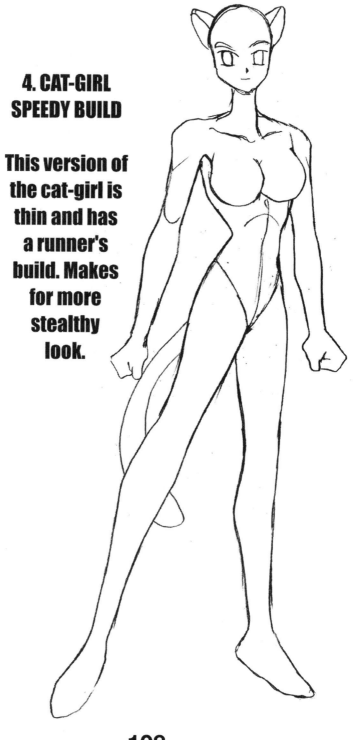

## DRAW A KAT-GIRL
### BODY TYPES

Cats have many types of patterns. I would suggest you pick one that you like personally. It can add a lot to your character if you choose a good body pattern, and it makes the character easy to identify over the years.

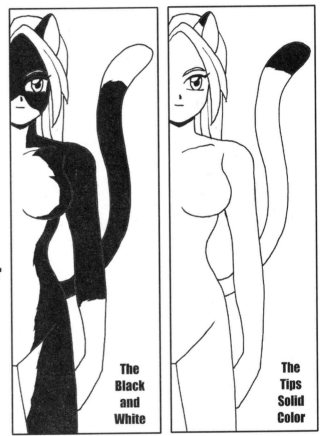

The Black and White

The Tips Solid Color

# HOW TO DRAW MANGA

## DRAW A KAT-GIRL
### BODY TYPES

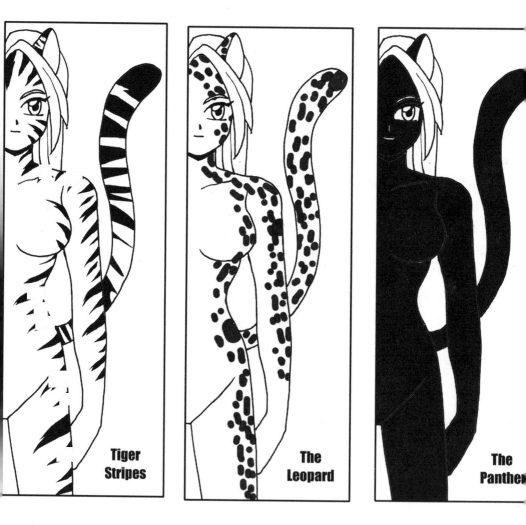

**Tiger Stripes**

**The Leopard**

**The Panther**

## DRAW A KAT-GIRL
### HEAD

THE MOST OBVIOUS PART OF THE CAT-GIRL IS THE HEAD. AS WE HAVE COVERED EARLIER, THE RULES REMAIN PRETTY MUCH THE SAME FOR DRAWING THE HEAD. HOWEVER, DURING THE PENCILSTAGE THERE ARE A FEW CHANGES THAT ARE NEEDED TO MAKE YOUR CAT-GIRL

### STEP ONE

PENCIL THE BASIC HEAD. YOU CAN ADD HUMAN EARS AT THIS STAGE IF YOU WISH. I HAVE DECIDED TO LEAVE THEM OFF TO GIVE THE CHARACTER A MORE CAT-LIKE APPEARANCE.

# HOW TO DRAW MANGA

## DRAW A KAT-GIRL
### HEAD

### STEP TWO
NOW PENCIL IN THE EARS.  EAR PLACEMENT IS VERY IMPORTANT AS THIS WILL BE THE
ONE THING THE READER WILL NOTICE RIGHT AWAY.

# HOW TO DRAW MANGA

## DRAW A KAT-GIRL
### HEAD

### STEP THREE
NOW INK THE SKETCH AND YOU'RE DONE!

# HOW TO DRAW MANGA

## DRAW A KAT-GIRL
### EYES

The eyes mirror the soul. More so in cat-girls. There are several approaches one can take on this. One is to simply do the large, dewy eyes of a typical manga female. Doing eyes this way gives the character a more human feel. The other is to do the more feline look. This makes the cat-girl more mysterious and alien. Either way can be used depending on what you intend to use the character for. I personally prefer a more human eye.

**HUMAN**  **CATTY**

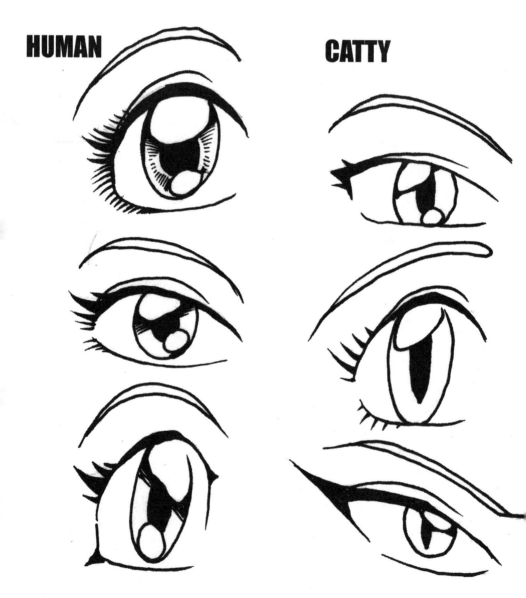

## DRAW A KAT-GIRL
### MOUTH AND NOSE

**The mouth can also be human or cat-like. Doing a more cat-like mouth usually means a bit more of a curve around the edges and a curve in the middle.**

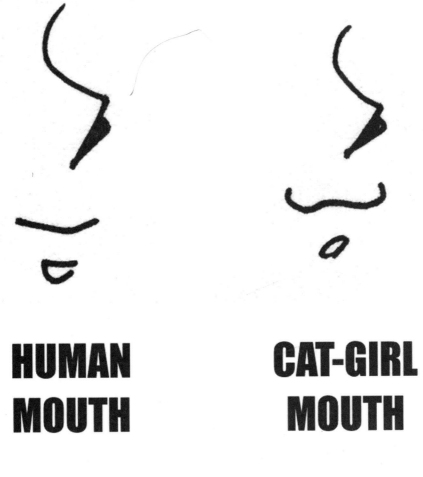

**HUMAN MOUTH**

**CAT-GIRL MOUTH**

## DRAW A KAT-GIRL
### EXPRESSIONS

**HAPPY**

**SAD or SERIOUS**

**CONTENT**

**TALKING**

## WHISKERS OR NOT WHISKERS

An option that one may choose is to add whiskers to the cat-girl. I tend to disdain their use, for it tends to make the cat-girl too catty. However, this is not to say they cannot be used. Try using them in your design phase and see how you like it.

## DRAW A KAT-GIRL
### HANDS AND PAWS

THERE ARE SEVERAL WAYS YOU CAN ARM YOUR CAT-GIRL. IT DEPENDS ON HOW YOU
WANT TO PRESENT YOUR CHARACTER.

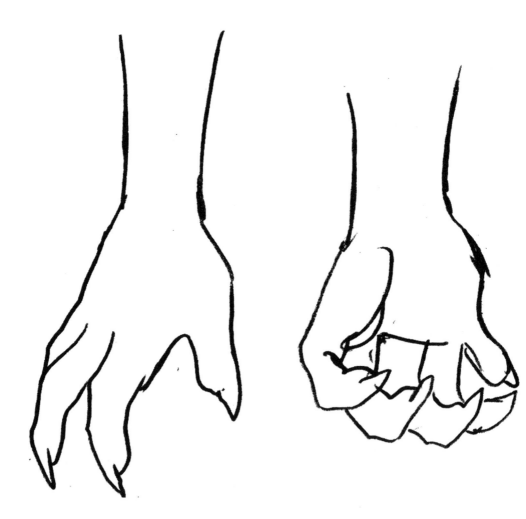

THESE HANDS ARE MORE HUMAN-LIKE, AND I TIPPED THEM WITH CLAWS. THIS MAKE
THEM MORE FIERCE, AND I WOULD USE THEM IF YOU WANT THE CHARACTER TO LOOK
MORE INTIMIDATING.

## DRAW A KAT-GIRL
### HANDS AND PAWS

THESE HANDS TEND TO BE MORE PAWLIKE AND MORE GENTLE. YOU CAN OPT TO TIP
THEM WITH CLAWS, BUT THAT IS UP TO YOU.

## DRAW A KAT-GIRL
### EARS

CAT-GIRL EARS ARE FAIRLY SIMPLE TO DO, BUT THEY CAN SAY A LOT. LOOKING AT TH
EARS, THE READER CAN ALMOST IMMEDIATELY IDENTIFY THE CHARACTER AS A CAT-GIRL
BY SHIFTING EARS ABOUT, YOU CAN CHANGE THE RANGE OF EMOTIONS EASILY.

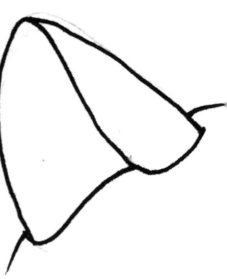

**Upright ears mean that
the character is alert.**

## DRAW A KAT-GIRL
### EARS

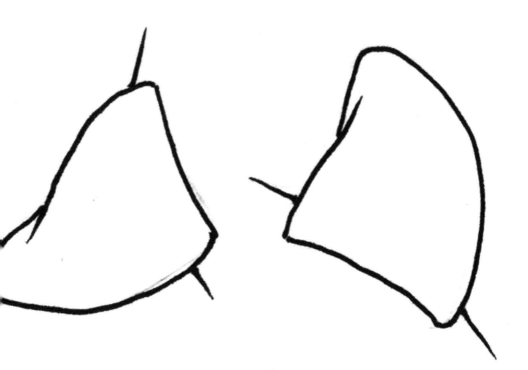

**Drooping ears means the
character is sad or depressed.**

## DRAW A KAT-GIRL
### EARS

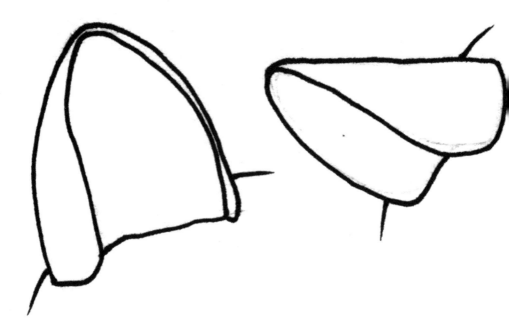

**A relaxed ear means
the character is at ease.**

## DRAW A KAT-GIRL
### TAILS

Adding the tail completes the cat-girl illusion. Usually, the tail follows the spinal cord and edges out. The tail can be used to give the character more flavor and can actually enhance her look.

## DRAW A KAT-GIRL
### TAILS

Adding the tail completes the cat-girl illusion.  Usually, the tail follows the spinal cord and edges out.  The tail can be used to giv the character more flavor and can actually enhance her look.

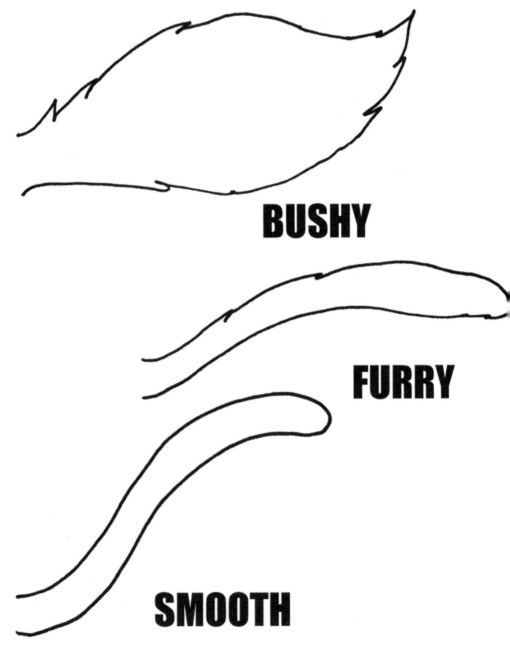

**BUSHY**

**FURRY**

**SMOOTH**

# HOW TO DRAW MANGA

## DRAW A KAT-GIRL
### TAILS

Now that you know how to draw the CATGIRL, try incorporating it in your next manga story! You won't regret it! MEOW!

## SMALL-BODIED TYPES

NE OF THE MORE BIZARRE ASPECTS OF MANGA IS THE DRAWING STYLE KNOWN AS
;D" OR "SUPER-DEFORMED." I CALL IT "SMALL-BODIED," THOUGH IT IS ALSO
ALLED "CHIBI." THIS IS USUALLY EMPLOYED TO CREATE AN INCREDIBLY CUTE
HARACTER OR TO MAKE A NORMAL CHARACTER LOOK LIKE IT HAS INHABITED A
HILD'S BODY. I CAN'T EXPLAIN IT, BUT IT IS A MAINSTAY OF MANGA AND I FIND
' STRANGELY APPEALING FROM AN ARTISTIC VIEWPOINT. HERE I WILL TRY TO
HOW HOW I HANDLE THESE IMPISH CHARACTERS.

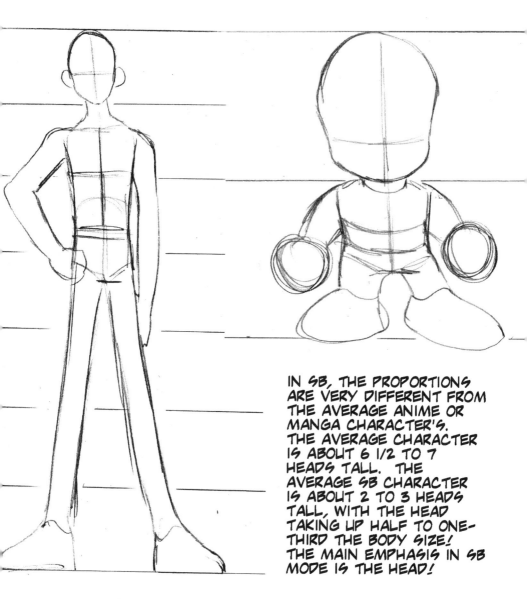

IN SB, THE PROPORTIONS
ARE VERY DIFFERENT FROM
THE AVERAGE ANIME OR
MANGA CHARACTER'S.
THE AVERAGE CHARACTER
IS ABOUT 6 1/2 TO 7
HEADS TALL. THE
AVERAGE SB CHARACTER
IS ABOUT 2 TO 3 HEADS
TALL, WITH THE HEAD
TAKING UP HALF TO ONE-
THIRD THE BODY SIZE!
THE MAIN EMPHASIS IN SB
MODE IS THE HEAD!

## SMALL-BODIED TYPES

SURPRISINGLY ENOUGH, THERE ARE RULES TO DRAWING EVEN IN SB MODE
EVEN THE RULES OF ANATOMY AND PROPORTION ARE IMPORTANT, AS WE
AS THE USUAL RULES OF PERSPECTIVE. IT IS NOT ENOUGH JUST TO DRA
SUPER-CUTE CHARACTERS. THEY STILL NEED TO INTERACT AND MOVE L
REAL CHARACTERS. IF THIS WERE A PEANUTS STRIP, YOU COULD GET AW
WITH SB ON A LIMITED BASIS, BUT THIS IS MANGA! AND WE DO THINGS
DIFFERENTLY HERE!

THERE ARE SEVERAL BODY TYPES
I USE WHEN I DRAW IN SB MODE:

## KID TYPE          MIDGET TYPE

KIND OF CHUNKY AND SQUAT.    I USE THIS TYPE TO SHOW
I USUALLY USE THIS TO        ADULT CHARACTERS IN CUT
DRAW CHILDREN.               BODIES.

## SMALL-BODIED TYPES

## THIN TYPE

## CHIBI TYPE

WHEN I WANT TO SHOW TEENS, I USUALLY USE THIS TYPE.

CHIBI TYPE IS USED AS A SORT OF GENERIC, CATCH-ALL TYPE OF BODY. I USUALLY USE THIS WHEN I NEED AN SB CHARACTER QUICKLY.

## SMALL-BODIED TYPES
### HANDS AND ARMS

DOING ARMS AND HANDS IS VERY SIMPLE IF YOU REMEMBER ONE BASIC RULE: CIRCLES! USING CIRCLES, YOU CAN CREATE ALMOST ANY HAND POSITION AND MAKE YOUR SB CHARACTER MORE DYNAMIC.

TUBE          SECTIONED

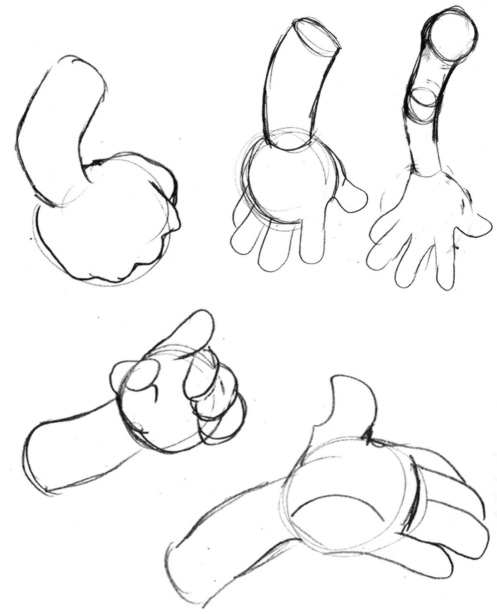

## SMALL-BODIED TYPES
### HANDS AND ARMS

FOR FINGERS, I IMAGINE LITTLE SAUSAGES AT THE END. FINGERNAILS ARE OPTIONAL. I USUALLY DRAW THE ARM IN SECTIONS. FOR THE REST, I USE THE TUBE-TYPE ARM.

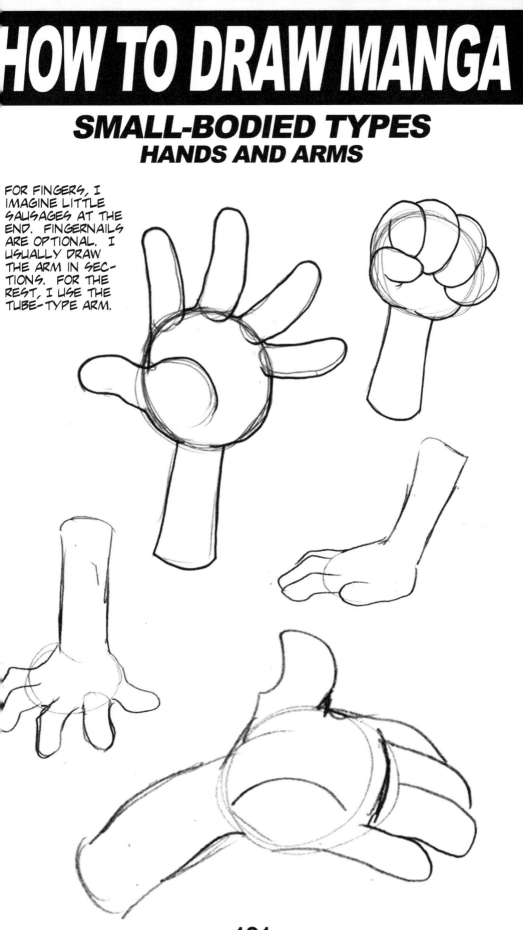

## SMALL-BODIED TYPES
### LEGS AND FEET

SIMILARLY TO ARMS AND HANDS, THE MAIN THING TO REMEMBER ABOUT FEET IS OVALS. YOU CAN DRAW THE FEET AND TOES USING A SERIES OF OVALS. AGAIN, WHEN I DRAW THE THIN TYPE OF BODY, I USE SECTIONED LEGS AND FEET.

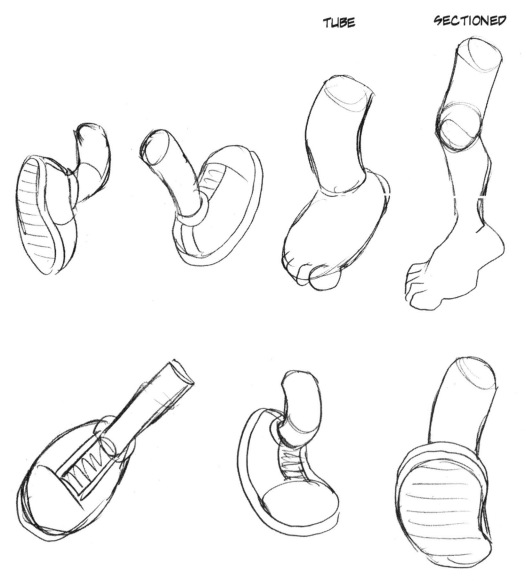

TUBE

SECTIONED

## SMALL-BODIED TYPES

I: SKETCH A BASIC ROUGH OUTLINE STARTING WITH THE HEAD AND BODY TYPE.

133

## SMALL-BODIED TYPES

2: SKETCH IN THE ARMS AND LEGS.

# HOW TO DRAW MANGA
## SMALL-BODIED TYPES

3: SKETCH
IN THE
FINGERS
AND FEET.

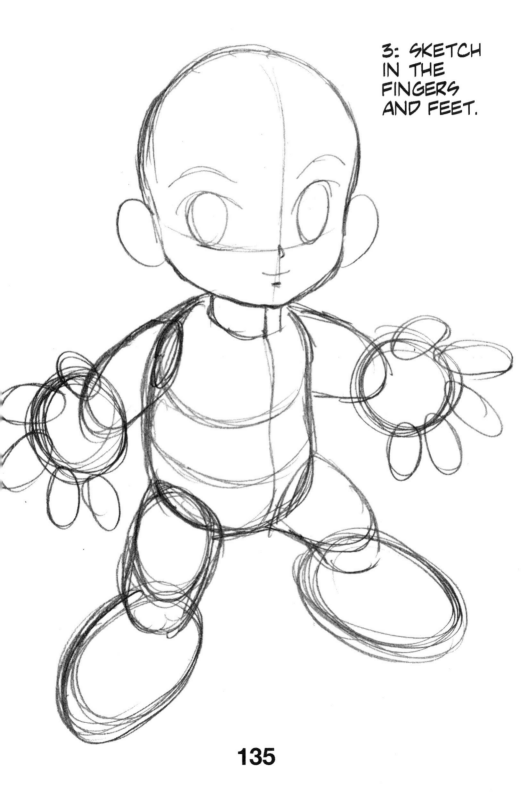

## SMALL-BODIED TYPES

4: ADD IN DETAILS.

# HOW TO DRAW MANGA

## SMALL-BODIED TYPES

5: INK THE
FINAL FIGURE.

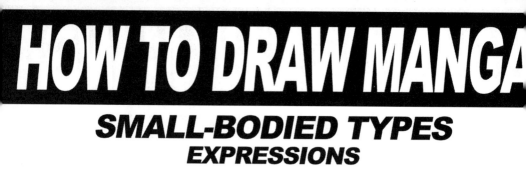

## SMALL-BODIED TYPES
### EXPRESSIONS

OKAY, ON TO THE NEXT LESSON!

I GOT SOME MORE VARIED EXPRESSIONS FOR YOU TO PORE OVER AND PRACTICE ON.

THERE ARE MORE EXPRESSIONS THAN THE USUAL BUG-EYED AND WIDE MOUTHED ONES. IN THE NEXT PAGES, I WILL SHOW YOU A NUMBER OF THEM.

**138**

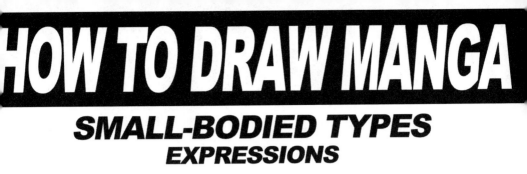

# HOW TO DRAW MANGA

## SMALL-BODIED TYPES
### EXPRESSIONS

HMM...
SUSPICION?
DOUBT?
SKEPTICISM?

THIS EXPRESSION
COVERS THOSE AND
THEN SOME!

SLIGHTLY
SCHEMING

A SMALL SMILE
AND A DEVIOUS
URN OF THE EYES
IS ALL IT TAKES

**139**

## SMALL-BODIED TYPES
### EXPRESSIONS

### OVERWHELMING SURPRISE

THE CHIBI
FIGURE HELPS
A LOT

### ON THE VERGE OF CRYING

SOMETIMES
A HARD EXPRESSION
TO DRAW.

## SMALL-BODIED TYPES
### EXPRESSIONS

SADNESS TO
THE POINT
OF CRYING
OR
SADLY
SYMPATHETIC.

**BAWLING OUT!**

(STREAMS OF
TEARS IS A
STANDARD
OF MANGA
STORYTELLING)

## SMALL-BODIED TYPES
### EXPRESSIONS

A GROWN MAN WEEPING LIKE A BABY IS AN UNUSUAL SOURCE OF HUMOR. SOMETIMES, THE UNEXPECTED IS A MOST EFFECTIVE WAY OF CONVEYING COMEDY.

ONCE AGAIN, THE RIVERS OF TEARS IS EMPLOYED TO EXAGGERATE THE EFFECT.

SNORING!

SURPRISE!!!

OR... KEPT AWAKE

142

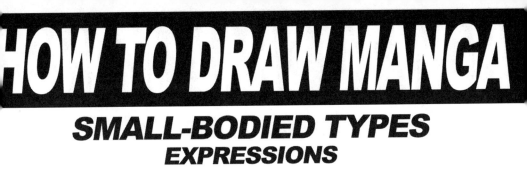

# HOW TO DRAW MANGA

## SMALL-BODIED TYPES
### EXPRESSIONS

UNEXPECTED
SURPRISE

OR

SUDDEN
EMBARASSMENT

ARGUMENTATIVE

LOUD REPLY

OR

SHOUTING A WARNING

## SMALL-BODIED TYPES
### EXPRESSIONS

CONNIVING
AND
GOSSIPING

CONCEIT
AND
ARROGANCE

# HOW TO DRAW MANGA

## SMALL-BODIED TYPES
### EXPRESSIONS

BASHFUL
SMILE
(AW GEE...)

WINK!

145

## SMALL-BODIED TYPES
### EXPRESSIONS

BURRRP!

HOT RETORT

## SMALL-BODIED TYPES
### EXPRESSIONS

"LOOK OUT
-- A WARNING"

SIMMERING ANGER

HAIR LOOKS FLAMELIKE

## SMALL-BODIED TYPES
### EXPRESSIONS

"AN UNPLEASANT
DISCOVERY"

BOREDOM
MAKING SNIDE REMARKS
OR
INSINUATING

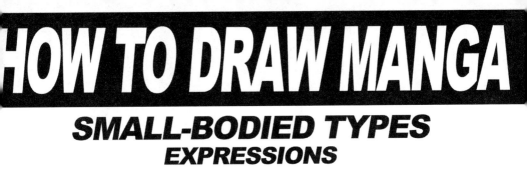

# HOW TO DRAW MANGA

## SMALL-BODIED TYPES
### EXPRESSIONS

SCHEMING
AND
PLOTTING

HOPPING MAD
YELLING OUT LOUD

## SMALL-BODIED TYPES
### EXPRESSIONS

CONSTERNATION

VOWING
VENGEANCE!

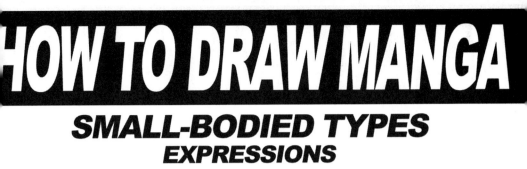

# HOW TO DRAW MANGA

## SMALL-BODIED TYPES
### EXPRESSIONS

DRUNK WITH
POWER
OR...
HAVING
DELUSIONS
OF GRANDEUR!

BLATANT
REFUSAL

OR

DENIAL

## SMALL-BODIED TYPES
### EXPRESSIONS

POPPING EYES!

BUG
EYED
SURPRISE!

IN LOVE,
"BEING SWEET"
OR ENAMORED

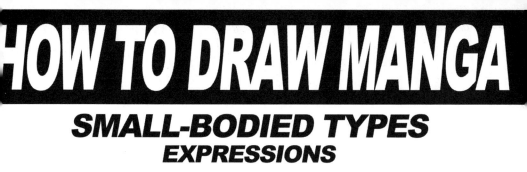

# HOW TO DRAW MANGA

## SMALL-BODIED TYPES
### EXPRESSIONS

CAUGHT OFF GUARD!

SHOCKING SURPRISE!

## SMALL-BODIED TYPES
### EXPRESSIONS

LARGE BUG EYED EXPRESSION COMBINE WITH THE LARGE TEETH IS A POPULAR EXPRESSION FOR PAIN IN MANGA.

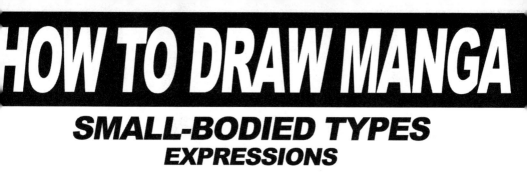

# HOW TO DRAW MANGA

## SMALL-BODIED TYPES
### EXPRESSIONS

ACCUSING

NYEEE!

## WARDROBE

WARDROBE IS EVERYTHING! WITHOUT IT, WE'D BE WEARING NOTHING! CHARACTERS' WARDROBE REFLECTS MANY ASPECTS ABOUT WHAT TYPE OF PEOPLE THEY ARE.  MOST IMPORTANTLY, THE OUTFITS WORN BY YOUR CHARACTERS WILL TELL THE READER WHAT ERA YOUR CHARACTERS RESIDE IN.  FOR EXAMPLE, IF YOU WERE TO ILLUSTRATE A STORY THAT TOOK PLACE AT THE TURN OF THE 20TH CENTURY, THERE WOULD DEFINITELY BE MANY DRASTIC FASHION DIFFERENCES.

TO THE LEFT, WE HAVE A GIRL IN SWIMWEAR. BIKINIS WEREN'T INVENTED AS OF THE DATE OF OUR STORY...SO HAVING HER IN ONE WOULD TAKE AWAY THE BELIEVABILITY OF HER RESIDING IN THE EARLY 1900S...EVEN THE SWIMSUIT I DREW HERE IS VERY RISQUE FOR THE TIME!

THE SECOND DRAWING IS VERY INACCURATE FOR THE TIME PERIOD, ALTHOUGH THE READER MIGHT NOT BE AWARE OF IT. TAKE THE TIME TO REFERENCE CLOTHING OF THE PERIOD IN WHICH YOU ARE ILLUSTRATING AND YOU WON'T BE CHEATING THE READER, PLUS YOU'LL BE MAKING YOUR DRAWING MORE AUTHENTIC TO THE READERS WHO ARE AWARE OF SUCH DETAILS!

# HOW TO DRAW MANGA

## WARDROBE
### DETAILS

WHEN DRAWING FASHIONS FROM A CERTAIN PERIOD, IT IS CRUCIAL THAT YOU FIND GOOD REFERENCE MATERIAL IN REGARDS TO IT. ONLY THEN WILL YOUR WARDROBES HAVE THE LOOK OF AUTHEN-TICITY THAT YOU'RE GOING FOR. THE KEY IS TO PUT YOUR CHARACTERS IN THE ENVIRONMENT THAT SURROUNDS THEM AND NOT TO CONTRADICT THAT WITH WARDOBE THAT IS ENTIRELY OUT OF PLACE FOR THAT ERA...UNLESS YOUR CHARACTERS ARE TIME-TRAVELLERS!

## WARDROBE
### DETAILS

A LOT OF THE HIGH FASHION OR "HAUTE COUTURE" OF THE EARLY 1900'S HAD A GREAT DEGREE OF DETAIL AND ORNATENESS. ILLUSTRATING THESE DETAILS WILL GIVE YOUR DRAWINGS EVEN GREATER RICHNESS AND BELIEVABILITY.

# HOW TO DRAW MANGA

## WARDROBE
### DETAILS

WHEN DRAWING FASHIONS FROM A CERTAIN PERIOD, IT IS CRUCIAL THAT YOU FIND GOOD REFERENCE MATERIAL IN REGARDS TO IT. ONLY THEN WILL YOUR WARDROBES HAVE THE LOOK OF AUTHENTICITY THAT YOU'RE GOING FOR. THE KEY IS TO PUT YOUR CHARACTERS IN THE ENVIRONMENT THAT SURROUNDS THEM AND NOT TO CONTRADICT THAT WITH WARDOBE THAT IS ENTIRELY OUT OF PLACE FOR THAT ERA...UNLESS YOUR CHARACTERS ARE TIME-TRAVELLERS!

## WARDROBE
### DETAILS

Day Wear 1900–1902

1901

1902

1902

1900

1902

1902

## WARDROBE
### DETAILS

THE MORE YOU REFERENCE AND STUDY A PARTICULAR
SUBJECT, THE BETTER UNDERSTANDING YOU'LL HAVE
OF THE SUBJECT, AND THEN YOU CAN TAKE SOME
CREATIVE LIBERTIES AND DESIGN THINGS IN ACCORD-
ANCE TO THOSE PRINCIPLES.

# HOW TO DRAW MANGA

## BASIC PERSPECTIVE

## BASIC PERSPECTIVE
### HORIZON LINE

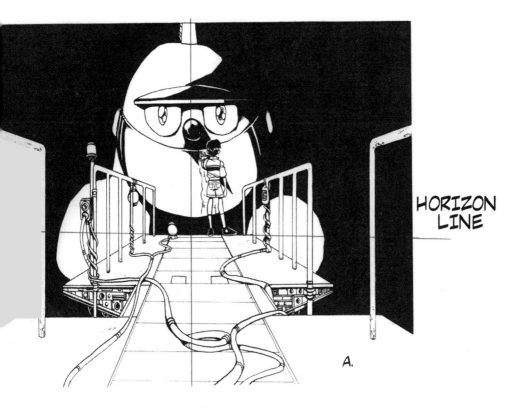

HORIZON
LINE

A.

IMPORTANT NOTE TO REMEMBER:
THE HORIZON LINE IS THE VERY
FOUNDATION OF PERSPECTIVE.
IT CAN BE A VERY POWERFUL
TOOL IN DRAWING AND IS THE
BASIS FOR ALL REALISTICALLY
RENDERED DRAWING. IT WORKS
IN FINE ART AS WELL AS IN
MANGA, SO IT IS IMPORTANT
TO MAKE NOTE OF IT!

EXAMPLE A:
HERE I WANTED
TO SHOW SCALE
BETWEEN THE
FOREGROUND
OBJECT AND
THE BACKGROUND
OBJECT.

## BASIC PERSPECTIVE
### HORIZON LINE

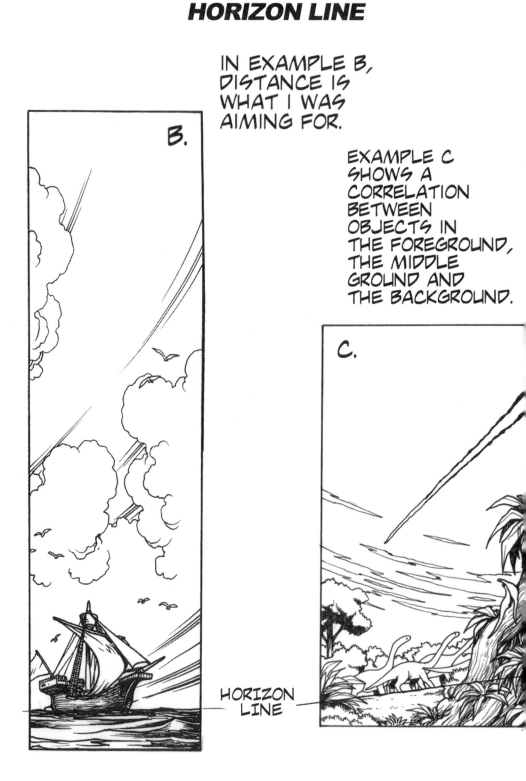

IN EXAMPLE B, DISTANCE IS WHAT I WAS AIMING FOR.

EXAMPLE C SHOWS A CORRELATION BETWEEN OBJECTS IN THE FOREGROUND, THE MIDDLE GROUND AND THE BACKGROUND.

B.

C.

HORIZON LINE

## BASIC PERSPECTIVE
### HORIZON LINE

BY USING THE HORIZON LINE
IN EXAMPLE D, YOU CAN ALSO
USE A FORCED PERSPECTIVE.

## BASIC PERSPECTIVE
### HORIZON LINE

IN DRAWING, PERSPECTIVE IS IMPORTANT IN
REALISTIC ART OR DRAMATIC STORYTELLING.

HORIZON
LINE

THE HORIZON LINE: THIS IS THE LINE THAT
APPEARS AS YOU LOOK OUT INTO THE DISTANT
HORIZON.  IT SEPERATES LAND FROM SKY.

## BASIC PERSPECTIVE
### HORIZON LINE

NORMAL EYE VIEW

THIS HORIZON LINE IS ALWAYS THERE WHEN YOU STAND ON A LEVEL FIELD. THIS LINE CAN BE BLOCKED BY OBJECTS OR DISTORTED BY LIGHT OR HEAT.

AT TIMES THE HORIZON WILL BE ONLY PARTLY VISABLE AS IN THE ILLUSTRATION. IMAGINE THE HORIZON LINE STRETCHING BEYOND THE OBSTRUCTIONS.

## BASIC PERSPECTIVE
### HORIZON LINE

IN PERSPECTIVE, IT IS IMPORTANT TO ESTABLISH THE VIEWER
IN RELATION TO THE HORIZON LINE, AND IT SHOWS THE EYE
LEVEL TO THE CHARACTER IN RELATION TO THE DRAWING.

Ⓐ

### THE BIRD'S-EYE VIEW

THIS VIEW TAKES THE
SUBJECT HIGH ABOVE
THE GROUND. PLACING
THE HORIZON HIGH
ENABLES ONE TO SEE
MORE OF THE GROUP.
THE HIGHER THE
HORIZON LINE, THE
HIGHER THE VIEWPOINT.
IT GIVES OBJECTS IN
THE DISTANCE A
SMALLER FEEL.

168

# BASIC PERSPECTIVE
## POINT OF VIEW

Ⓑ **THE WORM'S-EYE VIEW**

THIS PERSPECTIVE IS USED WHEN THE SUBJECT IS CLOSE TO THE GROUND OR WAY BELOW THE HORIZON LINE.  IT GIVES OBJECTS A LARGER FEEL.

## BASIC PERSPECTIVE
### POINT OF VIEW

EXAMPLES OF
BIRD'S-EYE VIEW
PERSPECTIVE...

USING THE BIRD'S-EYE
VIEW PERSPECTIVE GIVES
THE SPECTATOR A VISTA
OVER ALL THAT IS IN VIEW.
OFTEN IT IS USED TO
CONVEY VASTNESS,
SCALE AND TERRITORY.

170

## BASIC PERSPECTIVE
### POINT OF VIEW

IT HELPS PLACE
THE VIEWER IN AN AREA
THAT HE CAN BECOME
FAMILIAR WITH. IT
ALSO GIVES CHARACTERS
A SENSE OF PLACE.

# HOW TO DRAW MANGA

## BASIC PERSPECTIVE
### POINT OF VIEW

SIMPLE USE OF PERSPECTIVE
CAN HELP ESTABLISH TIME
AND PLACE. IT CAN GREATLY
INCREASE THE DRAMA OF ANY
GIVEN STORY.

# HOW TO DRAW MANGA

## BASIC PERSPECTIVE
### POINT OF VIEW

REMEMBER THAT ESTABLISHING
THE ENVIRONMENT CAN BRING
A NEW LEVEL TO THE STORY!

## BASIC PERSPECTIVE
### PICTURE WINDOW

BEFORE MAKING A PERSPECTIVE DRAWING, YOU MUST IMAGINE WHAT IS CALLED A "PICTURE WINDOW." THIS IS THE IMAGINARY WINDOW BETWEEN THE SPECTATOR AND THE RENDERING.

THIS ASPECT IS FUNDAMENTAL TO ALL OTHER ASPECTS OF PERSPECTIVE DRAWING.

## BASIC PERSPECTIVE
### LINE OF SIGHT

THE LINE OF SIGHT IS AN
IMAGINARY LINE THAT STARTS
FROM THE SPECTATOR AND
HEADS OFF INTO INFINITY. THE
LINE OF SIGHT IS USED BY THE
ILLUSTRATOR TO CREATE A
POINT OF REFERENCE.

## BASIC PERSPECTIVE

IN ORDER TO MASTER PERSPECTIVE, IT IS IMPORTANT
TO KNOW WHAT IS BEING TALKED ABOUT. BELOW IS A
GLOSSARY OF STANDARD PERSPECTIVE TERMS.

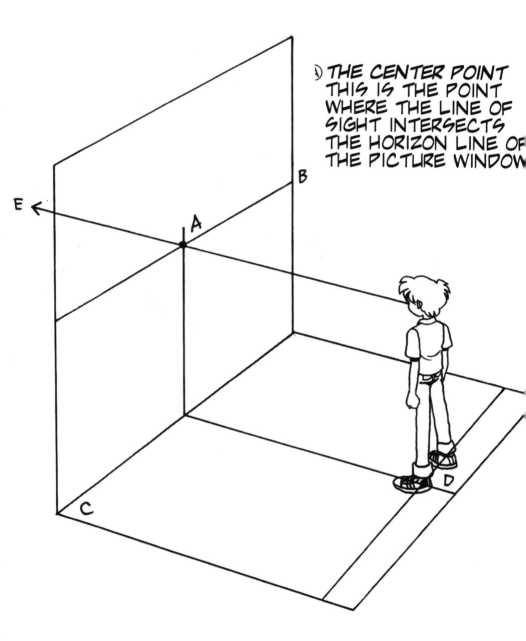

① THE CENTER POINT
THIS IS THE POINT
WHERE THE LINE OF
SIGHT INTERSECTS
THE HORIZON LINE OF
THE PICTURE WINDOW

## BASIC PERSPECTIVE

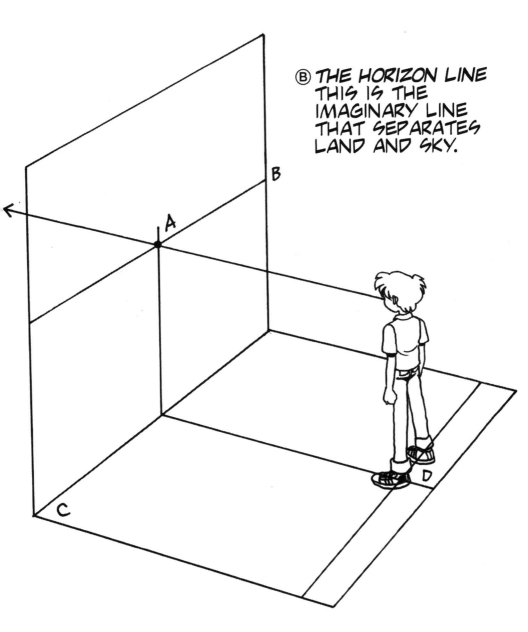

Ⓑ THE HORIZON LINE
THIS IS THE
IMAGINARY LINE
THAT SEPARATES
LAND AND SKY.

## BASIC PERSPECTIVE

© LAND LEVEL
THIS IS THE HORIZONTAL
LINE THAT SEPARATES
THE PICTURE WINDOW
AND GROUND LEVEL.

## BASIC PERSPECTIVE

Ⓓ SPECTATOR POINT
    THIS IS THE POINT ON THE GROUND LEVEL
    WHERE THE SPECTATOR STANDS AND FROM
    WHICH THE LINE OF SIGHT STARTS.

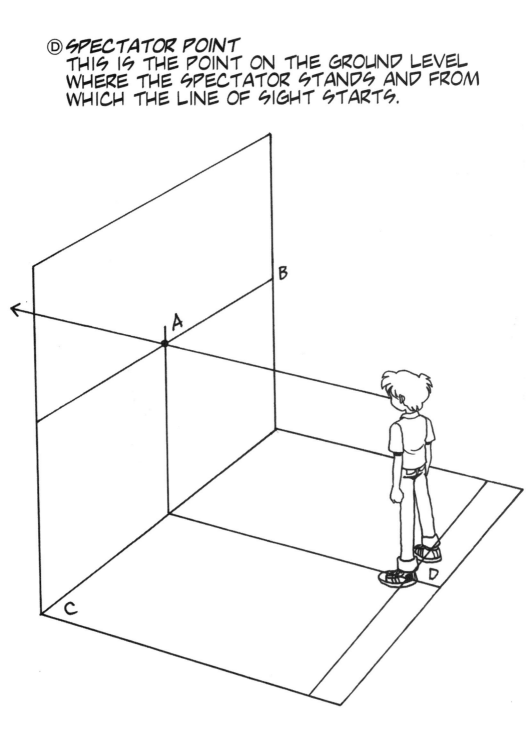

## BASIC PERSPECTIVE
### POINT OF VIEW

BY SWITCHING THE VIEWPOINT OF THE SPECTATOR, AN OBJECT IN VIEW CAN BE CHANGED. THE CLOSER THE VIEWER GETS TO AN OBJECT, THE MORE FORESHORTENING (SEE SIDE BOX) APPEARS WITHOUT BASICALLY ALTERING THE SIZE.

SPECTATOR VIEW           SPECTATOR DISTANCE

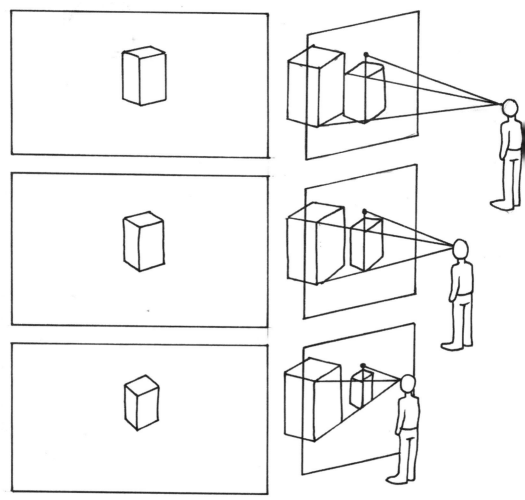

# HOW TO DRAW MANGA

## BASIC PERSPECTIVE
### FORESHORTENING

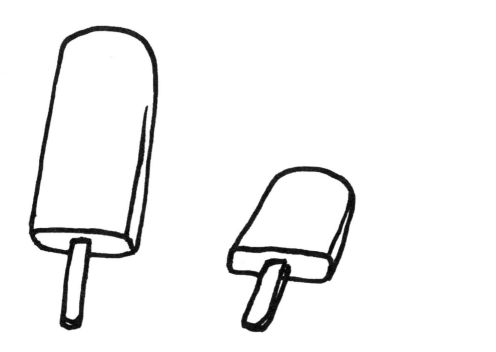

WHEN OBJECTS RECEDE INTO THE DISTANCE, THEY APPEAR SMALLER. EQUAL UNITS ALONG A RECEDING LINE APPEAR TO GET SMALLER OR "FORESHORTENED." IF THE AMOUNT OF PERSPECTIVE IS SLIGHT, THE RATE OF FORESHORTENING IS GRADUAL. IF IT IS GREAT, THEN THE RATE IS MORE DRAMATIC.

## BASIC PERSPECTIVE
### THE VANISHING POINT

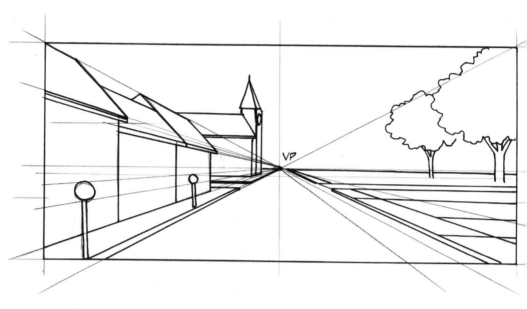

THE POINT ON THE LINE OF SIGHT WHERE ALL PARALLEL LINES RECEDING FROM THE SPECTATOR CONVERGE IS CALLED "THE VANISHING POINT." THIS IS THE POINT FROM WHICH ALL LINES OF PERSPECTIVE START.

## BASIC PERSPECTIVE
### ONE POINT PERSPECTIVE

HE ONE POINT PERSPECTIVE IS THE MOST BASIC FORM OF DRAWN PERSPECTIVE IN THAT ALL PARALLEL LINES RETREATING FROM THE SPECTATOR CONVERGE AT A POINT KNOWN AS THE VANISHING POINT (VP).

# BASIC PERSPECTIVE
## ONE POINT PERSPECTIVE

ALL LINES AND PLANES THAT
ARE SQUARE ON, PARALLEL TO,
ON THE PICTURE PLANE (AND THE
OBSERVER) REMAIN PARALLEL AND TO THEIR
TRUE SHAPE WITHOUT DISTORTION OR FORESHORTENIN

## BASIC PERSPECTIVE
### ABOVE AND BELOW

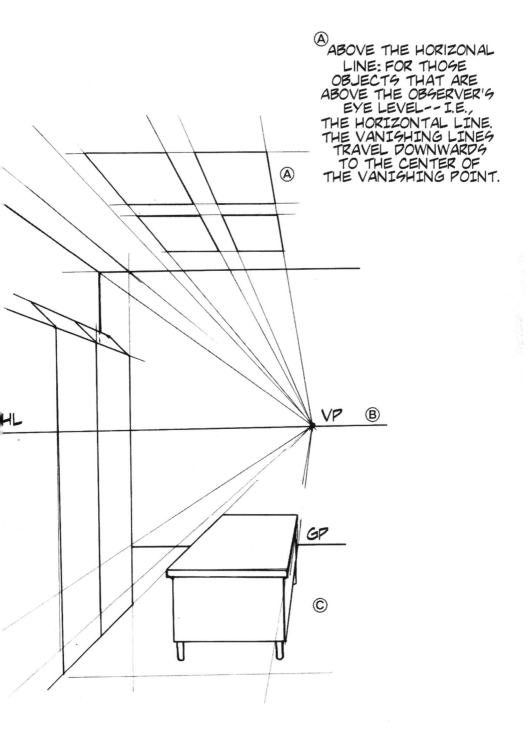

Ⓐ ABOVE THE HORIZONAL LINE: FOR THOSE OBJECTS THAT ARE ABOVE THE OBSERVER'S EYE LEVEL-- I.E., THE HORIZONTAL LINE. THE VANISHING LINES TRAVEL DOWNWARDS TO THE CENTER OF THE VANISHING POINT.

HL

VP Ⓑ

GP

Ⓒ

## BASIC PERSPECTIVE
### ABOVE AND BELOW

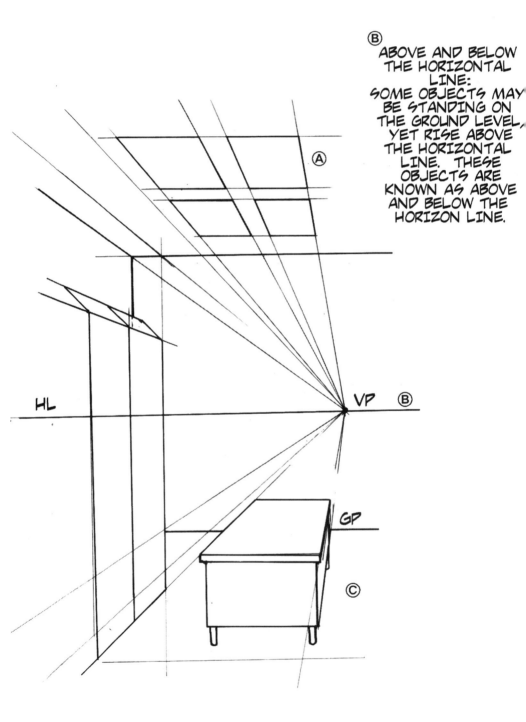

Ⓑ ABOVE AND BELOW
THE HORIZONTAL
LINE:
SOME OBJECTS MAY
BE STANDING ON
THE GROUND LEVEL,
YET RISE ABOVE
THE HORIZONTAL
LINE. THESE
OBJECTS ARE
KNOWN AS ABOVE
AND BELOW THE
HORIZON LINE.

## BASIC PERSPECTIVE
### ABOVE AND BELOW

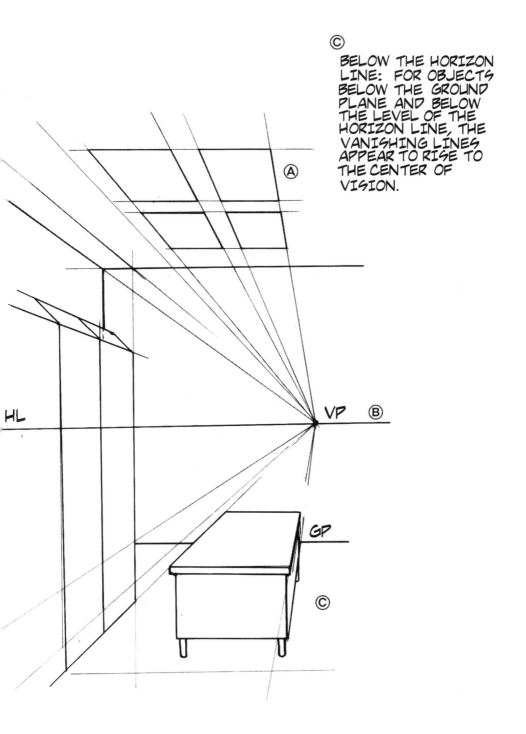

Ⓒ

BELOW THE HORIZON LINE: FOR OBJECTS BELOW THE GROUND PLANE AND BELOW THE LEVEL OF THE HORIZON LINE, THE VANISHING LINES APPEAR TO RISE TO THE CENTER OF VISION.

Ⓐ

HL

VP Ⓑ

GP

Ⓒ

# HOW TO DRAW MANGA

## BACKGROUNDS
### GRASS AND TREES

NOTHING ESTABLISHES TIME AND PLACE LIKE A WELL-CONSTRUCTED
BACKGROUND. IN USING BACKGROUNDS, YOU GIVE THE READER A POINT OF
REFERENCE ABOUT WHERE THE STORY IS AND HOW THE CHARACTERS
INTERACT. OVER THE COURSE OF MY YEARS OF DOING COMICS, I'VE NEVE
UNDERESTIMATED THE USEFULNESS OF A GOOD BACKGROUND TO ENHANCE
AND PROGRESS THE STORY! IN THIS SECTION, I WILL SHOW YOU HOW I D
SIMPLE BACKGROUNDS IN MY COMIC STORIES.

# HOW TO DRAW MANGA

## BACKGROUNDS
### GRASS AND TREES

GREETINGS! IN THIS PART OF "HOW TO DRAW MANGA," I WILL SHOW YOU HOW I DO OUTDOOR THINGS LIKE GRASS, ROCKS, TREES AND WATER!

## BACKGROUNDS
### GRASS AND TREES

DEPENDING ON WHAT YOU WANT TO DO WITH THEM, THESE SIMPLE ELEMENTS CAN GREATLY BRING A SENSE OF BELONGING TO THE STORY! BEING ABLE TO DO ORGANIC SCENES NOT ONLY HELPS FILL WHITE SPACE, IT CREATES MOOD!

## BACKGROUNDS
### GRASS AND TREES

PERSONALLY, I LIKE DRAWING BACKGROUNDS! IT'S VERY THERAPEUTIC FOR ME! READERS ARE FAMILIAR WITH THE NATURAL WORLD, AND IT HELPS THEM TO SEE WHAT KIND OF WORLD YOUR CHARACTER LIVES IN!

## BACKGROUNDS
### GRASS AND TREES

SO WITHOUT FURTHER ADO, LET'S ART MANGA!

## BACKGROUNDS
### GRASS

## GRASS

ONE OF THE MOST COMMON THINGS WE TAKE FOR
GRANTED IS GRASS. (NO, NOT THE STUFF YOU
SMOKE!) DRAWING GRASS CAN ADD A LEVEL OF
DETAIL THAT I THINK ENHANCES A GIVEN SCENE. IN
THIS SECTION, I WILL ATTEMPT TO SHOW YOU HOW I
DRAW THIS RATHER COMMON PLANT...

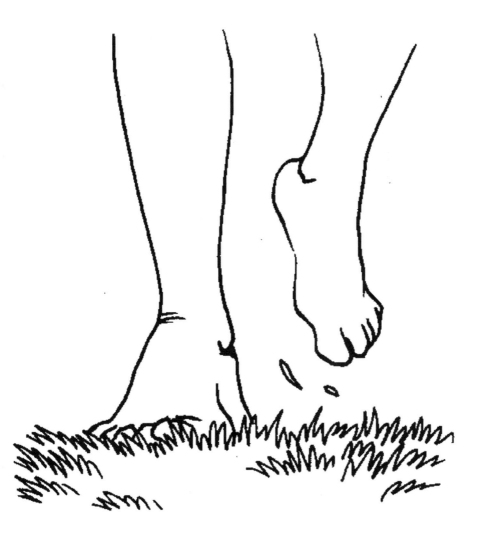

## BACKGROUNDS
### GRASS

## STEP 1

PLAN THE PLANE LEVEL.

## BACKGROUNDS
### GRASS

## STEP 2

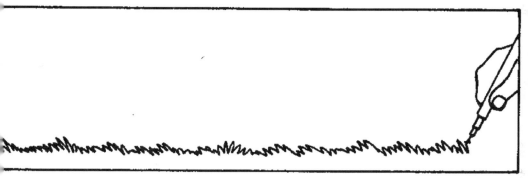

DRAW RANDOM BLADES USING
AN UP-AND-DOWN MOTION.
TRY TO VARY THE ROUGHNESS
A BIT SO THAT IT'S NOT
PERFECTLY UNIFORM.

## BACKGROUNDS
### GRASS

## STEP 3

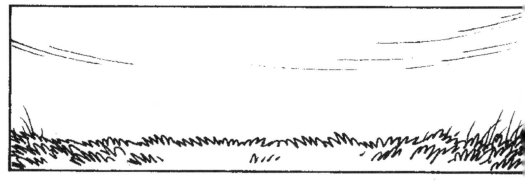

ADD PATCHES AT THE
SIDES TO GIVE IT DEPTH.

## BACKGROUNDS
### GRASS

HINT 1: GRASS LOOKS MORE REALISTIC IF IT OVERLAPS A FIGURE OR OBJECT.

NO OVERLAP

WITH OVERLAP

## BACKGROUNDS
### GRASS

HINT 2: WHEN DRAWING GRASS, ADDING MOVEMENT WILL GREATLY ENHANCE ITS DRAMATIC STORYTELLING.

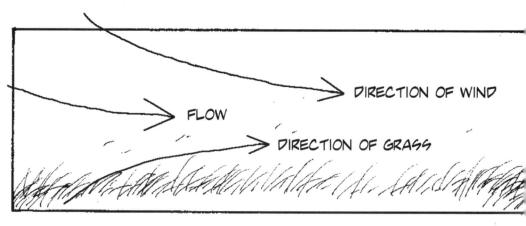

GRASS SHOULD BEND IN THE DIRECTION OF WIND FLOW.

## BACKGROUNDS
### GRASS

# PUTTING GRASS IN SILHOUETTE ALSO CAN CREATE DRAMA!

## BACKGROUNDS
### GRASS

SHADOWS ON GRASS MAKE FOR MORE INTERESTING
LAYOUTS. DO NOT FILL THE SHADOW IN SOLIDLY, BU
BREAK IT UP WITH A SERIES OF LINES.

USE A FINE POINT (I USED A .01 PIGMENT LINER)
TO DO THE SHADOW. MAKE SURE YOU INK IN THE
SAME DIRECTION AS THE SHADOW FALLS.

## BACKGROUNDS
### GRASS

PLAN YOUR SCENE AND USE
YOUR IMAGINATION TO FILL
IN RANDOM SPACES WITH
LIGHT STARTING POINTS
AND A SIMPLE
DOWNWARD
MOTION. DON'T
BE AFRAID TO
OVERLAP.

## BACKGROUNDS
### GRASS

HINT 3: THE MORE GRASS YOU DRAW, THE MORE OVERGROWN AN AREA IS PORTRAYED.

## BACKGROUNDS
### GRASS

HINT 4: WHEN DRAWING
GRASS HITTING A
SIDEWALK, USE THE
OVERLAP METHOD.

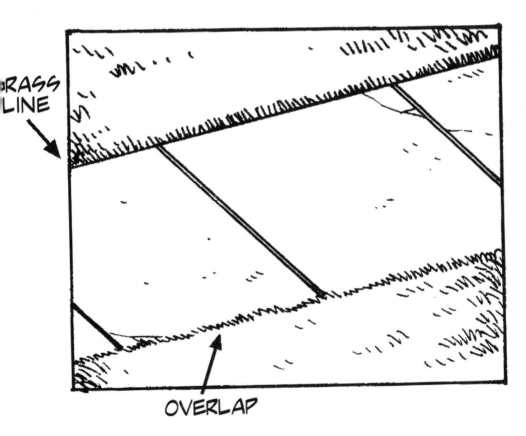

GRASS
LINE

OVERLAP

## BACKGROUNDS
### GRASS

# STEP 1

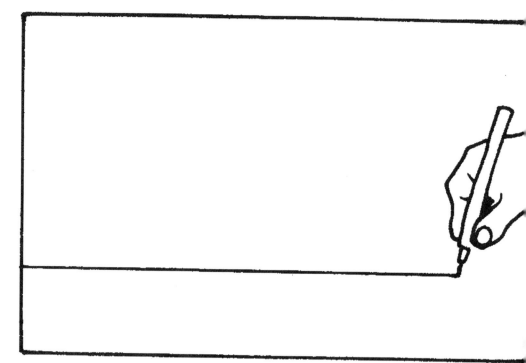

# PENCIL YOUR PLANE.

## BACKGROUNDS
### GRASS

# STEP 2

FOLLOWING YOUR PLANE, DRAW STALKS OF GRASS
USING BROKEN SPACES. A "DOWN-UP" STROKE IS
RECOMMENDED.

## BACKGROUNDS
### GRASS

HINT 5: WHEN DRAWING A GRASS LINE, USE A STRAIGHT EDGE AND MOVE YOUR PEN ALONG IT.

# HOW TO DRAW MANGA
## BACKGROUNDS
### GRASS

SOME EXAMPLES:

THE GRASS IS SUPPLEMENTED BY OTHER PLANTS. WHITE OPAQUE INK IS USED TO SHOW GRASS OVERLAP IN BLACK AREAS.

# HOW TO DRAW MANGA

IN THIS ILLUSTRATION, THE GRASS IS
DRAWN HUGE IN ORDER TO GIVE IT SCALE.

## BACKGROUNDS
### TREES

I THINK THAT I SHALL NEVER DRAW AN OBJECT AS LOVELY AS A TREE. I THINK THAT'S RIGHT...HECK, WHO CARES. THIS IS "HOW TO DRAW MANGA," NOT ENGLISH LIT! ANYWAY, I USE TREES QUITE OFTEN IN MY COMICS, NOT ONLY TO ADD ATMOSPHERE, BUT ALSO TO FILL "WHITE" SPACE. PLUS, THEY'RE FUN TO DO! HERE IS HOW I DO TREES.

**STEP 1**

DRAW A TRUNK WITH BRANCHES SPROUTING FROM THE MAIN TRUNK. TRY TO DRAW THE BRANCHES WITH LITTLE SYMMETRY.

**STEP 2**
INK IN THE
LEAVES AND
BRANCHES.

## BACKGROUNDS
### TREES

**STEP 3**

INK IN THE
SHADOWS
AND TRUNK
DETAILS.

## BACKGROUNDS
### TREES

# HINTS

DRAW LEAVES
SO THAT THEY
HAVE DEPTH.
TRY NOT TO
OVERDO IT!
KEEP THEM
IN A SEMI-
CIRCULAR
PATTERN.

THEY CAN BE USED TO
DO BUSHES AS WELL.

TREE TRUNKS LOOK
MORE REAL IF YOU
TEXTURE THEM.

## BACKGROUNDS
### LEAVES

THE PEN-BRUSH
TECHNIQUE

THIS TECHNIQUE IS
VERY EASY TO
MASTER, AND YOU
WILL FIND IT WORKS
IN A PINCH.

## BACKGROUNDS
### LEAVES

HE SECRET IS
GOOD BRUSH
ND STEADY
ONTROL. BE
AREFUL NOT
O OVERDO IT.

*HINT: THIS TECHNIQUE CAN BE
USED TO DO BUSHES AS WELL.

## BACKGROUNDS
### LEAVES

# STEP 1

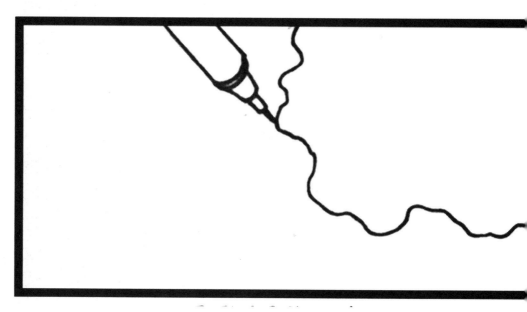

PENCIL A
PATTERN

## STEP 2

USE A BRUSH WITH A SHARP POINT. START WITH THE TIP OF THE BRUSH AND FAN OUT.

*ADD MORE BRANCHES IF NEEDED

## BACKGROUNDS
### LEAVES

## STEP 3

TECHNIQUE:
WHEN USING A PEN BRUSH
KEEP THE POINT INTACT.
DO NOT MASH YOUR POINT
IN. LET THE BRUSH MAKE
ITS IMPRESSION BY
SLIDING IT.

## BACKGROUNDS
### LEAVES

DRAWING LIFELESS OR LEAFLESS TREES IS FAIRLY EASY TO DO. JUST START WITH THE TRUNK AND RADIATE OUTWARDS.

REMEMBER, LITTLE BRANCHES ALWAYS RADIATE OUT OF LARGER BRANCHES. TRY NOT TO OVERDO IT OR THE BRANCH WILL LOOK UNNATURAL.

## BACKGROUNDS
### LEAVES

THE LIGHT SCRIBBLE EFFECT:

YOU CAN MAKE A TREE LOOK MORE
MATURE USING THIS METHOD. YOU
LITERALLY "SCRIBBLE" THE LEAVES
ON. IT IS MORE TIME-CONSUMING,
BUT THE EFFECT IS REALLY GOOD.

## BACKGROUNDS
### LEAVES

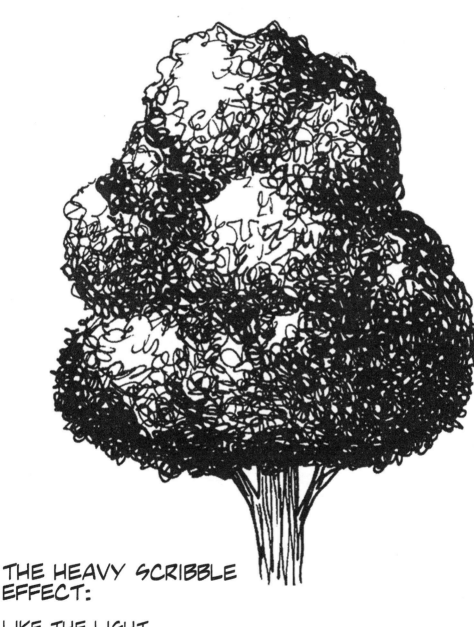

THE HEAVY SCRIBBLE
EFFECT:

LIKE THE LIGHT
SCRIBBLE EFFECT,
EXCEPT WITH
MORE SCRIBBLES.

## BACKGROUNDS
### LEAVES

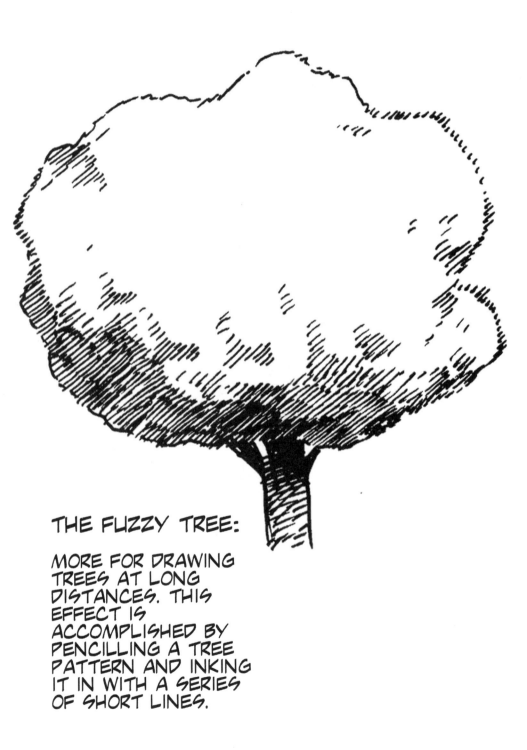

THE FUZZY TREE:

MORE FOR DRAWING
TREES AT LONG
DISTANCES. THIS
EFFECT IS
ACCOMPLISHED BY
PENCILLING A TREE
PATTERN AND INKING
IT IN WITH A SERIES
OF SHORT LINES.

## BACKGROUNDS
### LEAVES

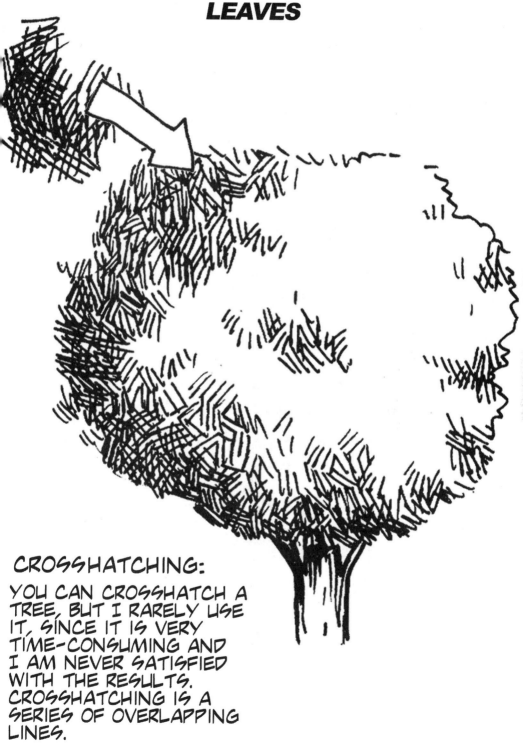

CROSSHATCHING:

YOU CAN CROSSHATCH A TREE, BUT I RARELY USE IT, SINCE IT IS VERY TIME-CONSUMING AND I AM NEVER SATISFIED WITH THE RESULTS. CROSSHATCHING IS A SERIES OF OVERLAPPING LINES.

## BACKGROUNDS
### TREE TRUNKS

THERE ARE 3 MAJOR TYPES I USE
TO DRAW TREE TRUNKS.

TYPE 1:

TEXTURED WITH VERTICAL
LINES.  THIS IS DONE BY
PICKING A LIGHT SOURCE
AND USING YOUR INKPEN
TO DRAW UNEVEN VERTIC
LINES.

224

# HOW TO DRAW MANGA

## BACKGROUNDS
### TREE TRUNKS

**TYPE 2:**

VERTICAL LINES WITH
HORIZONTAL LINES.
THIS GIVES A TREE
MORE PIZAZZ.

**HINT:** WHEN DOING
A TREE, CONSIDER
ITS LIGHT SOURCE.
THIS WILL HELP MAKE
YOUR SCENE MORE
DRAMATIC AND
REALISTIC.

## BACKGROUNDS
### TREE TRUNKS

**TYPE 3:**

VERTICAL LINE WITH FORKS. THIS ADDS SOME TEXTURE AND LOOKS MORE BARK-LIKE.

**HINT:**

YOU CAN COMBINE ANY OR ALL THREE OF THES TYPES TOGETHER! MIX & MATCH!

# HOW TO DRAW MANGA

# HOW TO DRAW MANGA

## WATER EFFECTS

WATER. IT IS THE STUFF OF LIFE AND IT CAN ADD LIFE TO YOUR MANGA STORY. OFTEN I WILL WORK IN THE ELEMENTAL ASPECT OF WATER IN ORDER TO GAIN A MORE DOWN TO EARTH FEEL. NOT ONLY IS WATER AN EQUALIZER IN THAT IT HELPS BRING FORTH THE NATURAL WORLD IT CAN ALSO EXUDE A CERTAIN SENSUALITY THAT CAN ADD SPICE TO YOUR STORY.

## WATER EFFECTS

PROFESSOR STEAMHEAD HERE TO TELL YOU THE THREE STATES OF WATER AND HOW IT APPLIES TO YOUR MANGA!

FIRST IS THE LIQUID STATE. THIS IS PROBABLY THE MOST COMMON STATE YOU WILL DRAW WATER IN. WATER IN THIS STATE IS CLEAR AND HAS MANY INTERESTING PROPERTIES AS WE WILL DISCUSS LATER IN THIS CHAPTER!

# HOW TO DRAW MANGA

## WATER EFFECTS

NEXT COMES
WATER AS A SOLID.
WHEN DRAWING IT IN THIS
STATE GIVE IT A TRANSPARENT
FEEL. DRAW THE OTHER
SIDE OF THE SOLID TO GIVE
IT DEPTH.

## WATER EFFECTS

NEXT COMES MY FAVORITE...WATER AS A GAS OR STEEEEAAAAM!! WHEN DRAWING A STEAM CLOUD GIVE IT SHAPE BUT INK IT LIGHTLY AS TO GIVE IT AN AIRY FEEL. PLACING OBJECTS INSIDE THE CLOUD SHOULD BE FOGGY AND HARD TO SEE.

# HOW TO DRAW MANGA

## WATER EFFECTS
### DRAWING RAIN

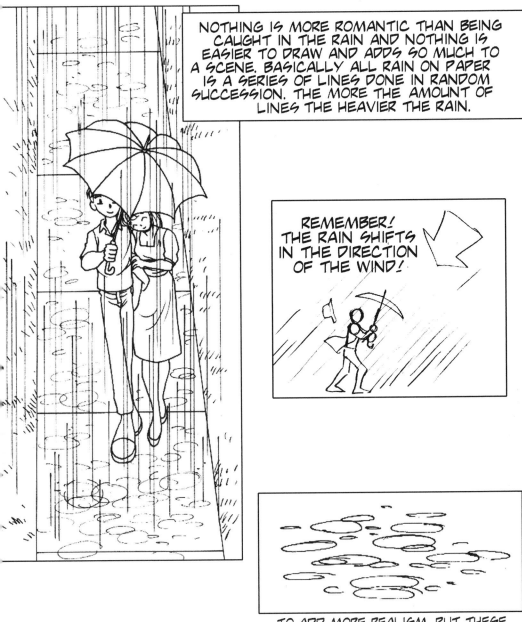

NOTHING IS MORE ROMANTIC THAN BEING CAUGHT IN THE RAIN AND NOTHING IS EASIER TO DRAW AND ADDS SO MUCH TO A SCENE. BASICALLY ALL RAIN ON PAPER IS A SERIES OF LINES DONE IN RANDOM SUCCESSION. THE MORE THE AMOUNT OF LINES THE HEAVIER THE RAIN.

REMEMBER! THE RAIN SHIFTS IN THE DIRECTION OF THE WIND!

TO ADD MORE REALISM, PUT THESE CONCENTRIC CIRCLES OF VARYING SIZES AS THEY HIT SOLID GROUND. IT ADDS A LOT TO A SCENE!

## WATER EFFECTS
### DRAWING RAIN

# LIGHT RAIN

# MODERATE RAIN

## WATER EFFECTS
### DRAWING RAIN

# HEAVY RAIN

## WATER EFFECTS

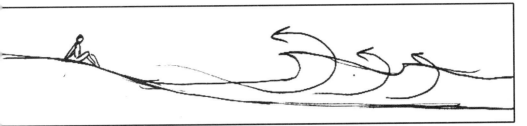

DRAWING WAVES ON A SEASHORE IS QUITE EASY AND FUN IF YOU REMEMBER SOME BASIC PRINCIPALS. WAVES COME IN AND ROLL OUT. THE TRICK IS TO CAPTURE THIS MOVEMENT.

WHEN ILLUSTRATING THE VIOLENT CRASH OF A WAVE YOU MUST FOLLOW THE MOTION OF THE WATER AS IT GOES AROUND OR THROUGH AN OBJECT.

## WATER EFFECTS

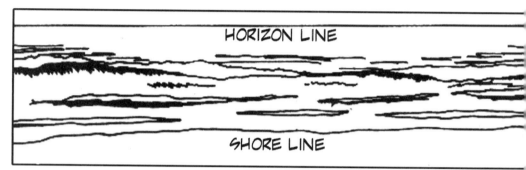

DRAWING A
BEACH LOOKING
OUT IS EASY
IF YOU ALTERNATE
THE WAVES AND
DRAW THE SHADOW
UNDER THE FOAM.

NOTE: WHEN DRAWING THE SHADOW OF
A WAVE USE A CURVED UP AND DOWN
MOTION TO GET THE BEST RESULTS.

238

## WATER EFFECTS

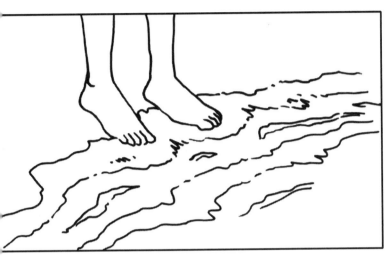

AS THE WAVES COME INTO THE SHORE IT IS IMPORTANT TO SEPERATE THE TWO ELEMENTS: LAND AND WATER.

UNDERNEATH THE WATER YOU WILL SEE THE SURFACE BREAK AND LIGHT SHINING THROUGH.

## WATER EFFECTS
### DRAWING WAVES

# STEP ONE:

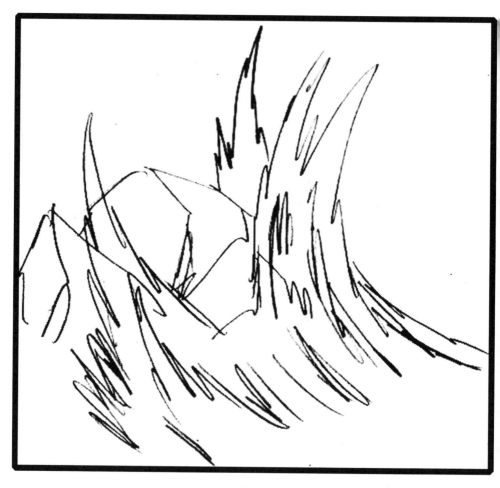

PENCIL IN THE OBJECT
AND THEN PENCIL IN THE
WAVES AS THEY HIT THE
OBJECT. BE SURE TO GIVE
IT IMPACT BY SPLITTING
THE WAVES INTO SEVERAL
ARMS.

# HOW TO DRAW MANGA

## WATER EFFECTS
### DRAWING WAVES

## STEP TWO:

INK THE WAVE AND ADD
SHADOWS WHERE IT IS
APPROPRIATE.

## WATER EFFECTS
### DRAWING WAVES

# STEP THREE:

TO ADD MORE SPRAY
USE THE PEN-WHITE
TOOTHBRUSH TECHNIQUE

# HOW TO DRAW MANGA

## WATER EFFECTS

A QUICK AND EASY WAY TO DRAW WAVES IS TO TAKE A SHARPIE AND DRAW THE SHADOWS OF A WAVE. MAKE THEM HEAVY NEAR THE EYE LEVEL AND LIGHTEN THEM AS THEY GO TOWARD THE HORIZON. THIS WORKS VERY WELL IN A PINCH!

## WATER EFFECTS

REMEMBER!
WATER MOVES
AROUND OBJECTS!
WATER CAN BE
GIVEN ITS OWN
CHARACTER!

WHEN WATER HITS
SOMETHING IT BREAKS
UP IN DROPLETS.

# HOW TO DRAW MANGA
## WATER EFFECTS

WATER FLOWS IN IRREGULAR PATTERNS. ADDING WATER DROPLETS ON SKIN CAN MAKE IT LOOK WET. BE SURE NOT TO OVERDO IT HOWEVER!

NEXT TIME YOU SEND A SWIMSUIT SUBMISSION... MAKE SURE YOU ADD WATER!!

## WATER EFFECTS

SOME
EXAMPLES
OF WATER
EFFECTS...

# HOW TO DRAW MANGA

## WATER EFFECTS

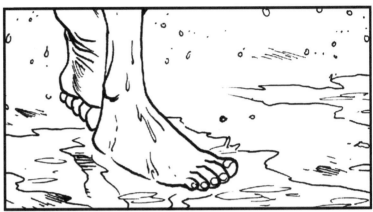

SOME
EXAMPLES
OF WATER
EFFECTS...

## WATER EFFECTS

EXAMPLES OF OPEN
WATER AND SHORES.

# HOW TO DRAW MANGA

## WATER EFFECTS

EXAMPLES OF OPEN
WATER AND SHORES.

# HOW TO DRAW MANGA

## SPECIAL EFFECTS

WE WILL BE STUDYING VARIOUS EFFECTS DEALING WITH EXPLOSIONS, IMPACTS, SMOKE TRAILS AND MANY OTHERS.

EXPLOSION

EXPLOSIONS ALWAYS RADIATE FROM A POINT OF ORIGIN.

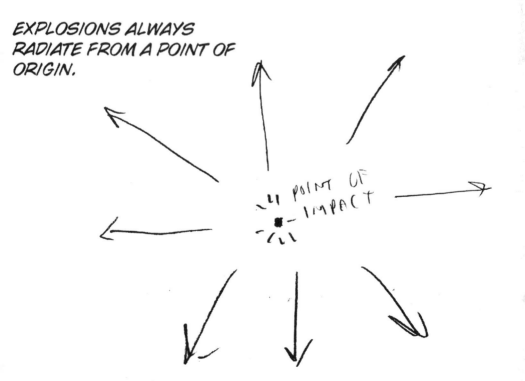

POINT OF IMPACT

## SPECIAL EFFECTS

OUTWARD ENERGY

THE ENERGY OF THE
BLAST LEADS FROM
THE POINT OF IMPACT
OUTWARDS EXCEPT IN
AREAS WHERE THERE IS
A GROUND OR THERE
ARE IMMOVABLE
OBJECTS IN THE
WAY.

P.O.I.

## SPECIAL EFFECTS

SLANTED POINTS OF IMPACT WILL CAUSE MOST
OF THE EXPLOSION TO GO THE SAME DIRECTION
AS ITS SOURCE. A SMALL PART OF THE EXPLOSION
ACTUALLY GOES BACK, BUT ONLY A SMALL PART.

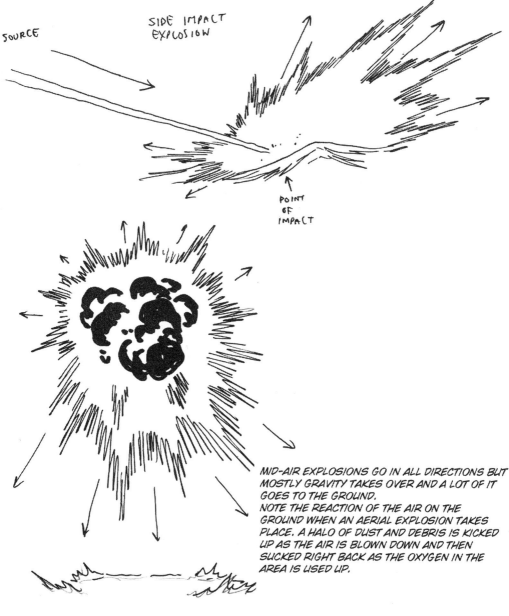

SOURCE

SIDE IMPACT EXPLOSION

POINT OF IMPACT

MID-AIR EXPLOSIONS GO IN ALL DIRECTIONS BUT
MOSTLY GRAVITY TAKES OVER AND A LOT OF IT
GOES TO THE GROUND.
NOTE THE REACTION OF THE AIR ON THE
GROUND WHEN AN AERIAL EXPLOSION TAKES
PLACE. A HALO OF DUST AND DEBRIS IS KICKED
UP AS THE AIR IS BLOWN DOWN AND THEN
SUCKED RIGHT BACK AS THE OXYGEN IN THE
AREA IS USED UP.

MID AIR EXPLOSION

## SPECIAL EFFECTS

SMOKE FROM THE
BARREL OF A CANNON
SLIGHTLY DIFFERS FROM
SMOKE PRODUCED AS
A RESULT OF A
FIERY EXPLOSION.

# HOW TO DRAW MANGA

## SPECIAL EFFECTS

EXPLOSIVE SCENES
COMBINED WITH SPEEDLINES
MAKE FOR SOME SPECTACULAR
SHOTS.

CREATING VOLUMES OF SMOKE
BEGINS BY USING A SERIES OF
CIRCLES AND SEMI-CIRCLES.
SKETCH THOSE LIGHTLY IN THEN
FOLLOW IT UP WITH RENDERING
USING A HEAVY BRUSH OR A THICK
PEN (LIKE A MARKER).

## SPECIAL EFFECTS

TO CREATE THE THICK BILLOWING EFFECT, NOTE HOW THE INNER PARTS OF THE SMOKE ARE LEFT INTENTIONALLY EMPTY (USUALLY WHERE THE FIRE IS).

DIRECTION OF WIND

LIGHTER ON TOP

DARK IN MIDDLE

LIGHTER ON BOTTOM

SMOKE FROM A DISTANCE IS RENDERED LOOSELY.
HERE, THE SMOKE BUILDS UP IN VOLUME AT THE MIDDLE,
BUT DISPERSES UPON REACHING HIGHER ELEVATIONS
WHERE THE SLIPSTREAM IN THE HIGHER STRATA
BLOWS FASTER.

## SPECIAL EFFECTS

A SMOKE TRAIL FROM A BURNING VEHICLE WIDENS AS A RESULT OF SLOW WIND DISPERSAL.

OILY BLACK SMOKE IS THE RESULT OF BURNING DENSE, ARTIFICIAL MATERIALS. MATERIALS LIKE OIL, TAR, PLASTICS, AND VARIOUS COMPOSITES BURN WITH BLACK SMOKE.

258

## SPECIAL EFFECTS

LIGHT SMOKE IS USUALLY PRODUCED BY BURNING
WOOD, PAPER OR ANY OTHER ORGANIC MATERIAL.

THERE IS ALSO A DIFFERENCE BETWEEN
SMOKE FROM LARGE FIRES AND SMOKE
FROM A CIGARETTE. NOTE THE GENTLE
WISPS CURLING UP FROM THE MOUTH OF
THE CHARACTER BELOW.

## SPECIAL EFFECTS

*SMOKE OR DUST CLOUD???*

*THERE IS A DIFFERENCE BETWEE SMOKE AND DUST CLOUDS. DUST CLOUDS ARE USUALLY RENDERED MORE LIGHTLY THAN FIRE SMOKE.*

STEAM IS LIGHTLY RENDERED -- MUCH LIKE DUST CLOUDS.
SOMETIMES THERE IS LITTLE DIFFERENCE BETWEEN THE TWO
EXCEPT THAT DUST CLOUDS USUALLY HAVE SMALL PARTICLES
OF DIRT PRESENT -- SIGNIFYING DUST MOTES.

DARK IN AREA
PRIMARY SMOKE
AREA

LIGHTER WITH
OVERLAPPING
SMOKE

FIGURE IN SMOKE

## SPECIAL EFFECTS

*MISSILE TRAILS! THE STUFF OF ANIME AND MANGA LEGEND! THIS IS ONE OF THE BEST STAPLES OF DRAWING MANGA AND THIS TIME AROUND, I'LL SHOW YOU HOW.*

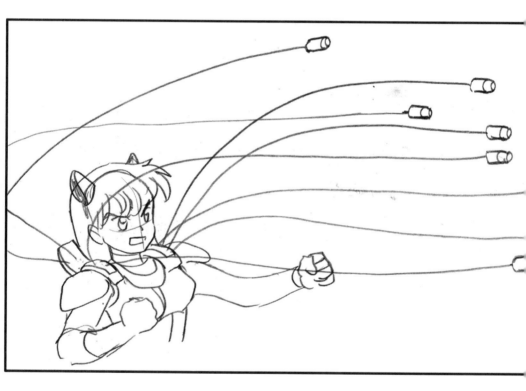

*FIRST, START WITH GENERAL DIRECTON LINES. THESE INDICATE THE TRAJECTORIES OF THE INDIVIDUAL MISSILES.*

NEXT, ADD EXHAUST FLAMES. MISSILES DON'T
FLY BY MAGIC, Y'KNOW! WELL, OKAY, SOMETIMES
THEY DO, BUT ONLY IN COMICS! MOST MISSILES
USE FUEL, AND THAT MEANS FLAME AND SMOKE!

## SPECIAL EFFECTS

EACH MISSILE TRAIL IS SIMPLY DRAWN WITH A SEMI-MEANDERING LINE SEEMINGLY UNTIL THEY LOCK ONTO A TARGET. WHEN THEY HOME IN ON THE TARGET, THEIR PATHS BECOME MORE STRAIGHT -- THEREBY PRODUCING THE EFFECT OF "HOMING IN".

# HOW TO DRAW MANGA

## SPECIAL EFFECTS

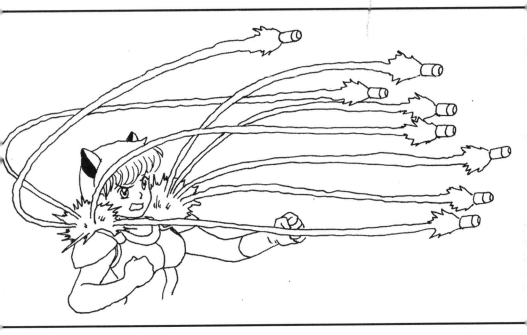

INK YOUR DRAWING AND YOU ARE DONE!

## SPECIAL EFFECTS

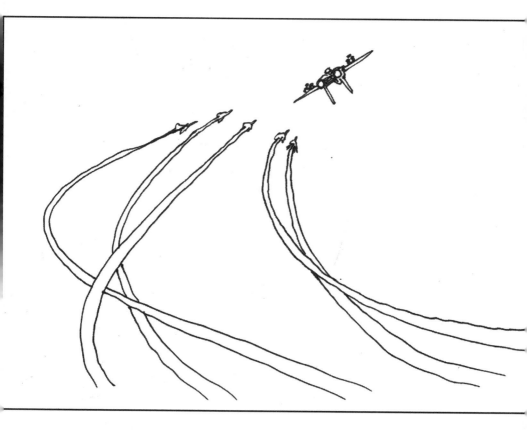

NOTE HOW THE THE SMOKE TRAIL WIDENS AS THE
MISSILE SHOOTS FORTH.
THIS IS A RESULT OF THE SMOKE TRAIL DISPERSING
IN THE WIND, BUT STILL MORE OR LESS DEFINED.

# HOW TO DRAW MANGA

## SPECIAL EFFECTS

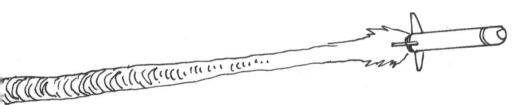

## SPECIAL EFFECTS

LAST BUT NOT LEAST,
SOME PRACTICAL USES!
COMBINED WITH THE ADEQUA
USE OF SPEEDLINES, YOU CA
CREATE QUITE EFFECTIVE
SCENES OF MASS MAYHEM!

## SPECIAL EFFECTS
### SPEED LINES

A LOT HAS BEEN SAID ABOUT THE USE OF SPEEDLINES IN MANGA, AND OUT OF ALL THE TECHNIQUES USED IN MANGA, SPEEDLINES ARE PERHAPS THE MOST PROMINENT AND CONTROVERSIAL!

BEFORE WE BEGIN, LET ME DEFINE WHAT "SPEEDLINES" ARE. TO ME, SPEEDLINES ARE LINES USED IN DRAWING TO EMPHASIZE MOVEMENT, SPEED, OR DRAMA! SPEEDLINES CAN BE USED TO VERY GOOD EFFECT IF EMPLOYED PROPERLY! HERE IS HOW I USE THEM!

THERE ARE SEVERAL WAYS TO APPROACH SPEEDLINES. THE FIRST THING YOU WILL NEED IS A GOOD RAISED-EDGE RULER (SEE ILLO. 1), A T-SQUARE, AND A ROLLING RULER. SINCE I USE A PIGMENT LINER DON'T REALLY WORRY ABOUT INK SPLOTCHES THAT OCCUR WITH A DIPPER INK QUILL.

## SPECIAL EFFECTS
### SPEED LINES

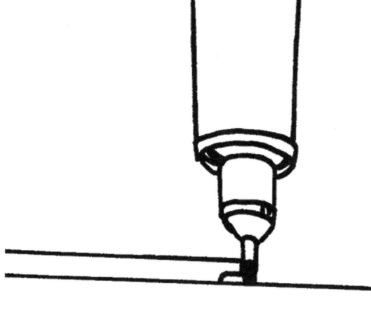

ILLO. 1
RAISED-EDGE RULER

## SPECIAL EFFECTS
### SPEED LINES

## SPECIAL EFFECTS
### SPEED LINES

WHEN USING A
ROLLING RULER
(MY FAVORITE
LINE TOOL),
FOLLOW THE
FLOW OF THE
RULER

## SPECIAL EFFECTS
### SPEED LINES

NOT TOO MUCH PRESSURE.
FOLLOW THE RULER EDGE.

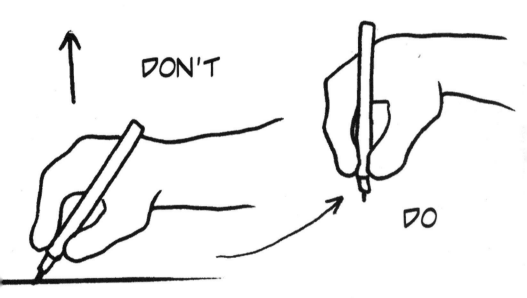

DON'T

DO

WHEN DRAWING THE LINE, DON'T
MERELY LIFT THE PEN UP, BUT
RELEASE THE TENSION IN ONE
FELL SWOOP!

## SPECIAL EFFECTS
### SPEED LINES

SPEEDLINES CAN BE USED TO GREAT EFFECT IN MANGA.
HERE ARE SOME SAMPLES OF SOME OF YOUR BASIC SPEEDLINES.

# TYPE:1

HORIZONTAL MEDIUM SPEEDLINES CAN BE USED TO
DENOTE SPEED, URGENCY, OR HIGH EMOTION.
THESE ARE DONE WITH A PIGMENT LINER WITH LINE
RANDOMLY SPACED AND BUNCHED.

# TYPE:2

HORIZONTAL MEDIUM EVENLY SPACED SPEEDLINES
ARE USED IN MUCH THE SAME WAY AS TYPE I BUT
LOOK MORE UNIFORM. THESE ARE DONE BY SPACING
I LINE FOR EVERY 3 OR 4 LINES BUNCHED TOGETHER.

## SPECIAL EFFECTS
### SPEED LINES

# TYPE:3

HORIZONTAL LIGHTLY SPACED SPEEDLINES ARE
USED TO CONVEY MINIMAL ACTION AND TO BREAK
UP WHITE SPACE.

# HOW TO DRAW MANGA

## SPECIAL EFFECTS
### SPEED LINES

TRY PRACTICING YOUR SPEEDLINES SO THAT YOU CAN GET A FEEL FOR THE PEN AND HOW MUCH PRESSURE YOU WILL NEED.

# TYPE:4

HORIZONTAL TIGHTLY SPACED SPEEDLINES ARE THE MOST TIME-CONSUMING, SINCE THEY REQUIRE DRAWING A LOT OF LINES IN ORDER TO BUNCH THEM TOGETHER AND GET THE DARK LINES. THIS IS USED AS THE ABOVE BUT IT ALL GIVES THE PANEL A SENSE OF URGENCY.

## SPECIAL EFFECTS
### SPEED LINES

WHEN DOING SPEEDLINES, TRY TO FOLLOW THE FLOW OF ACTION

WHEN A CHARACTER
MOVES HORIZONTALLY,
DRAW HORIZONTAL
SPEED LINES.

## SPECIAL EFFECTS
### SPEED LINES

WHEN A CHARACTER
IS MOVING VERTICALLY,
FOLLOW VERTICAL
SPEEDLINES.

## SPECIAL EFFECTS
### SPEED LINES

WHEN A CHARACTER
MOVES AT AN ANGLE,
FOLLOW THE LINES
OF PERSPECTIVE.

# HOW TO DRAW MANGA

## SPECIAL EFFECTS
### RADIAL SPEED LINES

## RADIAL SPEEDLINES AS PART OF THE ACTION

# HOW TO DRAW MANGA

## SPECIAL EFFECTS
### RADIAL SPEED LINES

## SHOWING RAPID MOVEMENT AND INTENSIT

## SPECIAL EFFECTS

EVENLY SPACED VERTICAL SPEEDLINES
USUALLY DENOTE MOOD
OR SADNESS.  THE SPACING
BETWEEN LINES SHOULD BE EVEN.

# HOW TO DRAW MANGA

## SPECIAL EFFECTS

RADIAL SPEEDLINES
USUALLY REPRESENT SURPRISE,
EXCITEMENT OR HAPPINESS.

# HOW TO DRAW MANGA

## SPECIAL EFFECTS

THIS EFFECT I CALL THE
RADIAL FRIZZ EFFECT. IT
IS ESSENTIALLY A SERIES
OF BROKEN LINES DRAWN
TO CREATE A RADIAL EFFECT.

## SPECIAL EFFECTS

THIS EFFECT IS THE STARBURST. ESSENTIALLY IT IS USE
TO SHOW COYNESS OR INNOCENCE. IT IS DONE BY
PENCILLING A CIRCLE AND DRAWING ALTERNATE LINES
AROUND IT.

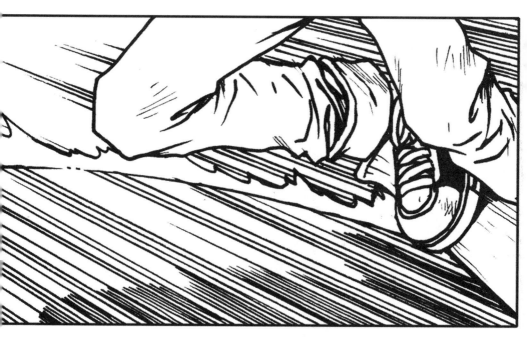

SHADOW SPEEDLINES ARE CREATED WHEN
YOU USE NORMAL SPEEDLINES THEN PENCIL
A SHADOW AND THEN INK MORE SPEEDLINES
IN ORDER TO CREATE A BROKEN SHADOW.

## SPECIAL EFFECTS

A COMMON EFFECT THAT I
USE IS CALLED THE OVERLA
SPEEDLINES. THIS IS WHER
SPEEDLINES OVERLAP INTO
THE ACTUAL DRAWING. IT I
A GOOD EFFECT BUT BE
CAREFUL NOT TO OVERDO

# HOW TO DRAW MANGA

## SPECIAL EFFECTS
### CURVED SPEEDLINES

CURVED SPEEDLINES
BY USING A CURVED RULER OR FRENCH CURVE, ONE CAN DO CURVED SPEEDLINES.
THIS IS USED TO ADD MORE MOVEMENT AND TO VARY THE LINE. HERE ARE THE VARIOUS TYPES.

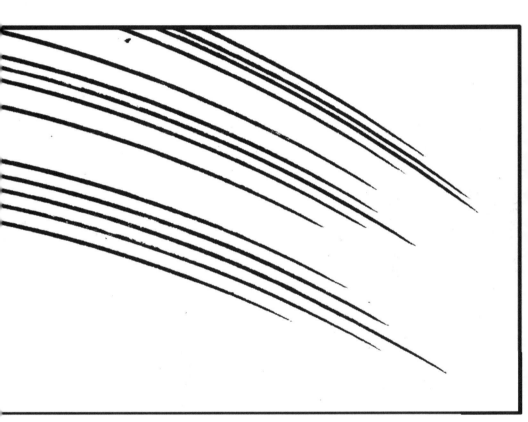

PARALLEL CURVES!
THESE HAVE NO CENTER POINT.
THIS IS ACHIEVED BY PULLING
THE CURVES DOWN PARALLEL.

## SPECIAL EFFECTS
### CURVED SPEEDLINES

CURVED LINES WITH A CENTER
POINT. NOTICE ALL THE LINES
GO TOWARDS A SINGLE POINT,
BUT THAT THEY DO NOT CONVERGE.

# HOW TO DRAW MANGA

## SPECIAL EFFECTS
### CURVED SPEEDLINES

OST OF THESE TECHNIQUES CAN EASILY BE
CHIEVED WITH THE USE OF A FRENCH CURVE.

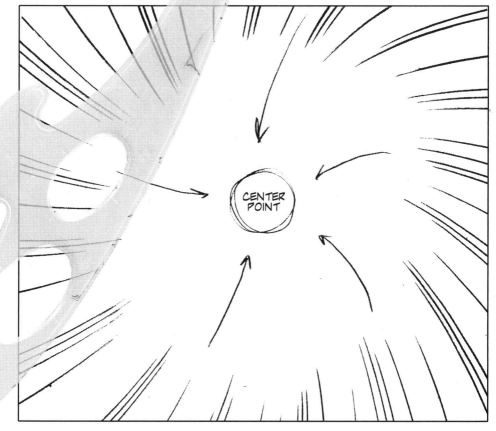

CENTER
POINT

RADIAL CURVED LINES
PICK A CENTER POINT AND RADIATE IN TOWARDS
IT USING YOUR CURVE TO FOLLOW THE CENTER POINT.

## SPECIAL EFFECTS

IN THIS PANEL SEVERAL SPEEDLINE EFFECTS ARE USED: THE TYPICAL, THE OVERLAP, THE FRINGE AND THE BLUR. THE FRINGE IS A SPEEDLINE I USE TO GIVE SOMETHING MOVEMENT VERY SUBTLY. IF YOU NOTICE, THE AIRBAG AREALA EMPLOYS HAS TINY SPEEDLINES AROUND THE EDGES. THIS CONVEYS MOVEMENT WITHOUT USING LARGE SPEEDLINES. THE BLUR IS THE TREES IN THE BACKGROUND. INSTEAD DRAWING SOLID TREES, I USED A LINE EFFECT FOLLOWING THE FLOW OF THE DESCENT. THIS IS SIMPLY ACHIEVED BY DRAWING THE LINE OVER AND OVER WITHOUT IT BECOMING SOLID.

SPEEDLINES CAN ALSO DENOTE LIGHT OR
BRILLIANCE. IT HELPS THE EFFECT IF YOU
PICK A LIGHT SOURCE AND CAST A SHADOW.

# HOW TO DRAW MANGA

## SPECIAL EFFECTS

# TO SPEEDLINE OR NOT TO SPEEDLINE

# HOW TO DRAW MANGA

## SPECIAL EFFECTS

## TO SPEEDLINE OR NOT TO SPEEDLINE

A LOT IS SAID ABOUT THE USE OF SPEEDLINES. HERE IS A
TYPICAL PANEL WITH AND WITHOUT SPEEDLINES. IN MY OPINION
WHILE THE FIRST PANEL IS ALL RIGHT, IT LACKS EXCITEMENT
AND MOVEMENT. PLUS THERE IS TOO MUCH "WHITE SPACE"
I SAY USE THEM IF YOU WANT!

## SPECIAL EFFECTS

## SPECIAL EFFECTS

# HOW TO DRAW MANGA

## SPECIAL EFFECTS

# HOW TO DRAW MANGA

## SPECIAL EFFECTS

# HOW TO DRAW MANGA

## PEN-WHITE TECHNIQUES

ONE OF THE MOST BASIC AND USEFUL MATERIALS YOU CAN HAVE FOR DOING MANGA IS PEN-WHITE. THIS IS NOT TO BE CONFUSED WITH WHITE INK THE DIFFERENCE IS THAT INK IS THINNER AND TENDS TO BE MORE TRANSPARENT. PEN-WHITE IS OPAQUE AND IS BETTER FOR DOING THINGS LIKE OUTLINING.

I USE DR. MARTIN'S PEN-WHITE. IT IS THE MOST CON-SISTENT IN TERMS OF OPACITY AND SOLUBILITY, AND IS QUICK-DRYING. A BOTTLE WILL GO A LONG WAY AND WILL NOT DRY OUT AS SOME BRANDS WILL DO.

## PEN-WHITE TECHNIQUES

SOME PEOPLE USE TECHNICAL PENS FOR PEN-WHITE, AND THAT'S FINE, BUT I THINK THAT THEY TEND TO CLOG VERY EASILY AND MUST ALWAYS BE WASHED OUT AFTER EVERY USE.

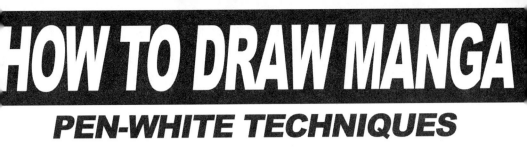

WATER

I GO MORE FOR THE STAN-DARD QUILL WITH A REALLY SHARP POINT, A REALLY SMALL BUT POINTY BRUSH, AND AN OLD TOOTHBRUSH. HAVE A SMALL CUP OF WATER NEARBY AS WELL.

## PEN-WHITE TECHNIQUES
### PREPARING YOUR BRUSH

# STEP ONE:

BEFORE STARTING WITH THE TOOTHBRUSH, IT IS IMPORTANT THAT THE BRISTLES BE SOFT AND FLEXIBLE.

DIP THE BRUSH IN WATER TO MOISTEN THE BRISTLES. THIS WILL ALLOW THE PEN-WHITE TO FLOW BETTER. DRY OFF EXCESS WATER.

NOTE: DO NOT USE TO BRUSH TEETH WITH AFTERWARDS. MAKE SURE IT IS A DEDI-CATED INK BRUSH!

## PEN-WHITE TECHNIQUES
### PREPARING YOUR BRUSH

# STEP TWO:

TAKE AN EYEDROPPER
AND DAB A FEW DROPS
OF PEN-WHITE ON THE
FRONT OF THE BRUSH.
TOO MUCH AND YOU'LL
GET A REAL MESS.

DRY OFF ANY EXCESS
WHITE, AS IT WILL
CLUMP TOGETHER AT
THE FRONT AND DROP
ONTO YOUR ARTWORK.

## PEN-WHITE TECHNIQUES
### QUICK & EASY STAR FIELD

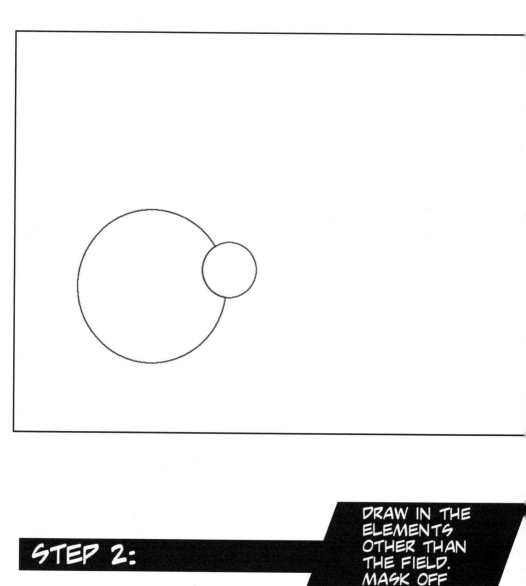

**STEP 2:**

DRAW IN THE ELEMENTS OTHER THAN THE FIELD. MASK OFF THAT AREA.

## PEN-WHITE TECHNIQUES
### QUICK & EASY STAR FIELD

**STEP 3:** BLACKEN IN THE AREA YOU WISH TO BE THE STARFIELD.

## PEN-WHITE TECHNIQUES
### QUICK & EASY STAR FIELD

**STEP 4:**

LIGHTLY USE YOUR TOOTH- BRUSH AND SPECKLE THE FIELD AREA.

## PEN-WHITE TECHNIQUES
### QUICK & EASY STAR FIELD

STEP 5: REMOVE THE MASK.

## PEN-WHITE TECHNIQUES
### QUICK & EASY STAR FIELD

## STEP 6:

AIRBRUSH ANY AREA TO ENHANCE. THIS STEP IS OPTIONAL.

## PEN-WHITE TECHNIQUES
### QUICK & EASY STAR FIELD

DOING THE TOOTHBRUSH TECHNIQUE IS
MORE AN ART THAN A SKILL. WHAT I
USUALLY DO IS HOLD THE BRUSH ABOUT
2-3 INCHES ABOVE THE ART TO GET
MAXIMUM EFFECT. OF COURSE, YOU CAN
HOLD IT CLOSER OR HIGHER TO GET DIF-
FERENT TYPES OF EFFECTS AND SPLAT-
TERS. I USUALLY HOLD THE BRUSH AT A
SLIGHT ANGLE AND PULL BACK WITH MY
THUMB, USING A LIGHT PRESSURE. IF
THE BRISTLES ARE MOIST, THE BRUSH
IS A LOT EASIER TO CONTROL. THIS
WILL MAKE YOUR THUMB WHITE, BUT
YOU MUST SUFFER FOR YOUR
ART. TRY EXPERIMENTING
WITH THIS AND SEE WHAT
EFFECT YOU GET!

THE KEY IS TO NOT OVERDO IT!!
IT IS ALWAYS BEST TO ERR ON THE
SIDE OF CAUTION. IT IS EASIER TO
ADD THAN TO SUBTRACT.

## PEN-WHITE TECHNIQUES

## USING THE BRUSH TECHNIQUE WITH BLACK INK

THE SAME TECHNIQUE CAN BE USED WITH BLACK INK. ALL KINDS OF EFFECTS CAN BE USED WITH THIS AND IT CAN GREATLY INCREASE DRAMA. WHEN DOING THIS, IT IS BASICALLY THE SAME PREP AS WITH PEN-WHITE, BUT YOU NEED TO BE CAUTIOUS, SINCE BLACK INK IS A LOT MESSIER AND YOU DON'T WANT TO USE IT ON MOM'S FAVORITE SOFA OR GOOD TABLE. IT IS BEST TO HAVE A NEWSPAPER AROUND THE EDGES TO CATCH ANY EXCESS SPLATTER

## PEN-WHITE TECHNIQUES
### OUTLINING A CHARACTER

ONE OF THE MORE
INTERESTING USES OF
PEN-WHITE IS TO BRING
OUT A CHARACTER AGAINST
A DARK BACKGROUND.

WHILE THIS IS NOT NECC-
ESSARY, IN SOME CASES
YOU WILL FIND THAT IT IS
NOT ONLY USEFUL, BUT
CAN GREATLY ENHANCE A
CHARACTER.  ALL YOU HAVE
TO DO IS PENCIL THE
CHARACTER AS YOU WOULD
NORMALLY DO, BUT PUT IN
THE LINES YOU WANT TO
OUTLINE IN INK.

**311**

## PEN-WHITE TECHNIQUES
### OUTLINING A CHARACTER

INK THE CHARACTER AND
BLACKEN IN THE DARK
AREAS.

## PEN-WHITE TECHNIQUES
### OUTLINING A CHARACTER

THEN WITH A BRUSH OR
QUILL GO OVER THE LINES
WITH PEN-WHITE UNTIL YOU
GET THE DESIRED EFFECT.

## PEN-WHITE TECHNIQUES
### OUTLINING A CHARACTER

THIS IS EXTREMELY USEFUL
FOR BRINGING FORWARD
AREAS YOU WANT TO
EMPHASIZE OR MAKING A
CHARACTER STAND OUT.
IT IS ALSO GOOD TO SHOW
FOLDS IN DARK CLOTHES OR
HIGHLIGHTS IN HAIR.

# HOW TO DRAW MANGA

## PEN-WHITE TECHNIQUES

## EXAMPLES of USE:

...ADDING EXTRA "LUMINANCE" TO A CANDLE...

<

> ...SHOWING HIGHLIGHTS ON BLACK CLOTHING...

# HOW TO DRAW MANGA

## PEN-WHITE TECHNIQUES

## EXAMPLES of USE:

< ...A BLAST TO THE DOME...OUCH.

JEREMY...

...A CLEAR NIGHT SKY... ∧

...PLEASE DON'T TRY THIS AT HOME!!!

>

# THE BIG HEAD SHOT

This type of cover is typically used to showcase strong emotion and to show people how well you can draw heads. Most of the time I find the "big head" shot is used when the artist is in a hurry to meet a deadline, though if done very well, it can be very impressive. I don't like using it too often, as it can be very boring layout-wise and it's too easy in many cases.

I used a large head shot for *Ninja High School* #81 because I wanted to show just what a badass Dog Supreme was without giving away the story inside. The trickle of blood from his nose was added to give the reader pause and make him ask, "What caused that?"

ADVANTAGES:
1. Easy to do in a pinch.
2. Conveys very strong emotions.
3. Easily attracts attention from a distance.
4. Simple layout.
5. A variation of this is known as "the multiple head shot." This is when many heads are used in a cover. (See *Silver Cross* #3 for example).

DISADVANTAGES:
1. Boring at times.

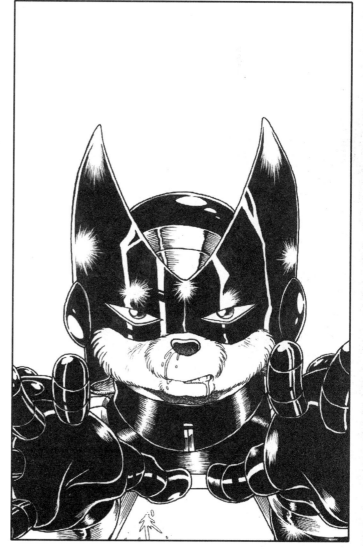

**2** # THE LARGE-SCALE ACTION SEQUENCE

One of the most exciting types of cover you can do is the large action sequence. Usually it is a part of the story that the cover artist finds particulary exciting. It is one of the most effective ways to tell the reader that there is something really cool going on inside this comic and that they must pick it up to find out what the comic is all about.

On this cover of *Mighty Tiny* #5 I opted to show the massive airship battle but juxtaposed the two main characters to show the how small they are in comparison to the events taking place. Large-scale sequences like this are very effective almost all the time and they are a lot of fun to do, but they are very time-consuming and can be difficult to lay out just right.

ADVANTAGES:
1. Always exciting and colorful.
2. Tells the story with one image.

DISADVANTAGES:
1. TIme-consuming.
2. Always a danger of giving away too much.
3. Difficult to lay out effectively.

# 3 THE SMALL-SCALE ACTION SEQUENCE

asically the same as the rge-scale version, but instead cuses mostly on characters acting to their surroundings recreating a part of the ory. A great way to show any characters at once doing sorts of things. Can be ry colorful and exciting if ne well. A slight variation this theme is the "multiple nding around sequence," en many characters are nply just standing. I usually oid these, as they can get ring pretty fast.

e cover of *Ninja High hool Yearbook* #13 shows st of the main *NHS V.2* aracters running around. is allowed me to showcase em in one fell swoop and pefully get the reader erested enough to pick up book based solely on what characters were doing.

DVANTAGES:
Showcase many characters nce.
Keeps the action personal.

SADVANTAGES:
Can appear too crowded.
Difficult to lay out.

## DESIGNING COVERS

### ④ THE LONE FIGURE

Certainly one of the best types of cover to employ is the lone figure shot. Elegent and direct, it tells the reader, "I am the focus of this story!" It also allows the artist to really get into the character and make that character really stand out. It's also a way for the artist to showcase his ability to draw the figure. It's often recommended to use a character who fits the mood of the story, though it can be used simply to show what the character can do. A static character usually portrays confidence, power, or high emotion. A character in action usually portrays ability and movement.

In this cover to *Ninja High School #86*, the figure is standing confident as a fleet of battleships moves overhead. By doing this, I show her as the unquestioned ruler of all she surveys!

ADVANTAGES:
1. Simple layout, but very effective.
2. Directly tells the reader who the main focus is on.

DISADVANTAGES:
1. Can be overused.

# HOW TO DRAW MANGA

## DESIGNING COVERS

# 5 THE CENTER FIGURE TRIUMPH SHOT

This type of cover is typically used to entice the reader with an "Oh, no!" reaction. Whenever a shot is used that shows the "bad guy" seemingly triumphant over the "good guy," that can't be good news. Effective in its ability to get the curious reader, it is for the most part a cliché in comics, because we all know the good guys will triumph in the end. However, it is fun to do, and believe it or not, still works on a basic level. This cover of *Zetraman: Revival* #1 was used because I felt the need show the old-fashionedess of the story. Also, since it dealt with a new origin of the Zetramen, it conveyed a sense of "out with the old and in with the new."

ADVANTAGES:
1. Still works and conveys a sense of nostalgia.
2. Simple layout.

DISADVANTAGES:
1. Can only be used sparingly.

## DESIGNING COVERS

# 6 THE MULTI-CHARACTER COLLAGE

This type of cover is typically used to show a lot of characters, usually with 1-3 individuals as the main focus. Simple layout-wise and effective as a way of showing the readers the varied cast, this type of cover is often used for a first issue or anniversary issue.

This cover for the color version of *Ninja High School* #1 was used in order to show the entire cast of the book in one fell swoop.

ADVANTAGES:
1. Shows the entire cast at once.
2. Simple layout.

DISADVANTAGES:
1. TIme-consuming if cast is complicated.
2. Cannot be used that often.

# HOW TO DRAW MANGA

## DESIGNING COVERS

### 1: LAYOUT AND DESIGN

Okay, here we go.

I've just plotted out the issue of *Ninja High School* #90 and I need to do a cover.

The first step is to decide what kind of cover I want. Since it is the start of a new storyline, I opt for the multi-character collage but limit it to 3 characters—Tomorrow Girl, Warrior Nun Areala and Ramen Rider—because I don't want to reveal too many secrets of the story.

Get some scratch paper and start sketching a layout. You will sometimes go through many such layouts before you become satisfied with one, or you may just have to do 1 or 2 if you are a seasoned pro like I am.

I find the first layout makes Tomorrow Girl look too confrontational and cuts across Ramen Rider. So I opt to have TM have her arm on her chest and give her a more innocent look.

Once you have decided on the layout, you go to the pencil stage.

LAYOUT 1

LAYOUT 2

# HOW TO DRAW MANGA

## DESIGNING COVERS

## 2: ROUGH PENCIL STAGE

At this stage, you start pencilling the final version of your cover.

# HOW TO DRAW MANGA

## DESIGNING COVERS

## 3: FINAL PENCILLING STAGE AND INKING

## DESIGNING COVERS

At this stage, I make a change in the story—Ramen Rider is dropped and Little Hu is included. I erase Ramen Rider and insert Little Hu.

## DESIGNING COVERS

Now all the characters are inked. I don't do a background, opting to let the colorist fill in the space. Once you are done inking, erase the pencils.

## DESIGNING COVERS

### THE FINISHED COVER!

# HOW TO DRAW MANGA

*BEN DUNN ASKS YOU...*

## SO YOU WANNA BE IN COMICS?!

*...AND HE SHOWS YOU HOW!*

# HOW TO DRAW MANGA

SO YOU WANT TO BE A COMIC BOOK SUPERSTAR?
AH, DON'T WE ALL! BUT FIRST THINGS FIRST! HOW
DO I BREAK IN TO THIS GLORIOUS FIELD? WELL, IT
ALL STARTS WITH THE SUBMISSION PROCESS! A
PATH TO GLORY THAT COULD ONE DAY MAKE YOU
A LEGEND IN YOUR OWN TIME! SO COME ALONG
AS WE CHASE THE DREAM!

## PART 1:
## SUBMITTING DIRECTLY TO A COMIC COMPANY

### STEP 1:
### PICK YOUR PROFESSION!
WHERE DO YOUR TALENTS LIE? DO YOU WANT TO BE A WRITER, PENCILLER, INKER, LETTERER, ETC. OR ALL OF THE ABOVE? PICK YOUR STRENGTHS AND ROLL WITH IT!

### STEP 2:
### WHAT'LL IT BE?
HOW DO YOU WANT TO WORK FOR A COMPANY...
A. WORK FOR HIRE:
    WORKING ON A PARTICULAR COMPANY'S TITLES AND CHARACTERS.

OR

B. CREATOR FOR HIRE:
   WORKING ON YOUR OWN CREATION FOR A
   PARTICULAR COMPANY.

EACH HAVE THEIR PROS AND CONS:
WORK FOR HIRE—
PRO: STEADY PAY IF YOU'RE CONTRACTED
      FOR A BOOK.
CON: YOU DON'T OWN THE RIGHTS TO THE
      STORIES OR CHARACTERS.
CREATOR FOR HIRE—
PRO: YOU OWN THE PROPERTY! ALL THE CHARACTERS
      STORIES, AND RIGHTS TO MARKET THEM, ETC.
CON: UNRELIABLE, AND IRREGULAR PAY, UNLESS
      YOU'VE ESTABLISHED YOURSELF AS HAVING
      A RELIABLE FAN BASE.

## STEP 2:
## REFINE THAT PORTFOLIO!

ONCE YOU'RE DONE FIGURING OUT WHAT IT IS YOU WANT TO FOCUS ON, START A PORTFOLIO! A PORTFOLIO IS A SAMPLE OF YOUR WORK THAT SHOWCASES YOUR TALENT TO THE PEOPLE THAT MAY POTENTIALLY GIVE YOU WORK, SO MAKE SURE YOU INCLUDE ONLY THE WORK THAT YOU FEEL IS THE BEST REPRESENTATION OF YOUR TALENT. IT IS ALSO A GOOD IDEA TO INCLUDE ANY PROFESSIONALLY PUBLISHED WORK IN YOUR PORTFOLIO; THIS SHOWS THAT YOU ARE FAMILIAR WITH WORKING WITH A PUBLISHER AND THAT YOU HAVE WORKED PROFESSIONALLY.

THINGS TO KNOW ABOUT ASSEMBLING YOUR PORTFOLIO:

1. USE ONLY YOUR BEST PIECES.
2. IF YOU HAVE A LARGE VARIETY OF WORK, MAKE SURE YOU ORGANIZE IT BASED UPON A CERTAIN THEME, SUCH AS KEEPING ALL YOUR SEQUENTIAL COMIC BOOK PAGE SAMPLES TOGETHER.
3. INCLUDE PUBLISHED SAMPLES OF YOUR WORK, IF ANY.
4. PRESENT YOUR PORTFOLIO IN A CLEAN AND ORGANIZED MANNER; DON'T CARRY AROUND A STACK OF BENT, TORN-UP PICTURES. BE NEAT. AND SHOW 'EM THAT YOU'RE A PROFESSIONAL!

NOTE!

SUBMITTING ART:

BEFORE YOU SUBMIT ART TO A PARTICULAR PUBLISHER, IT IS WISE TO STUDY WHAT THE PUBLISHER PUBLISHES! I WOULDN'T RECOMMEND SHOWING ARTWORK TO A PUBLISHER THAT CONSISTS MOSTLY OF SUPERHERO ART IF THAT PUBLISHER DOESN'T PUBLISH SUPERHERO COMICS. THAT IN MIND, GEAR YOUR SUBMISSION TOWARD THE TYPICAL GENRE OF TITLES THAT COMPANY PUBLISHES.

PIN-UPS VS. SEQUENTIAL PAGES:
COMIC COMPANIES ARE IN THE BUSINESS OF TELLING STORIES
FROM PANEL TO PANEL. SO ANY ASPIRING COMIC ILLUSTRATOR
SHOULD FILL HIS PORTFOLIO UP WITH PAGES OF SEQUENTIAL
ART. IF IT'S FULL OF PIN-UPS, IT DOESN'T SHOW AN EDITOR
THAT YOU CAN TELL A SEQUENTIAL STORY. HOWEVER, IF YOU
CAN DRAW PANEL-TO-PANEL PAGES WELL, IT'S ALMOST CERTAIN
TO AN EDITOR THAT YOU CAN PROBABLY DRAW A GOOD PIN-UP
OR COVER. IF YOU ABSOLUTELY HAVE TO SHOW HOW GREAT
YOU ARE AT DOING PIN-UPS AND WANT TO INCLUDE THEM WITH
A SUBMISSION OR A PORTFOLIO, MAKE SURE THE SEQUENTIAL
PAGES FAR OUTNUMBER THE PIN-UPS.

# HOW TO DRAW MANGA

STEP 3
SUBMIT!
LET THE PUBLISHER SEE YOUR GUSTO!
IT'S TIME TO LET A COMPANY SEE YOUR SUBMISSION AND
MARVEL AT YOUR CREATIVE POTENTIAL. THE FIRST THING TO
DO IS INQUIRE ABOUT A PARTICULAR COMPANY'S ALL-
IMPORTANT "SUBMISSION GUIDELINES"! THESE TELL YOU
EXACTLY THE TYPE OF WORK THEY'RE LOOKING FOR, HOW
MANY EXAMPLES THEY'D LIKE TO SEE, AND MOST IMPORTANTLY,
WHO TO SEND THEM TO!
START BY WRITING TO A COMPANY AND ASKING THEM FOR A
COPY OF THEIR SUBMISSION GUIDELINES. MOST COMPANIES'
ADDRESSES CAN BE FOUND IN THEIR BOOKS. LOOK FOR THE
PARTICULAR BOOK'S COPYRIGHT INFORMATION.

NOTE: IN THIS "AGE OF THE
INTERNET," MANY COMPANIES
POST THEIR CONTACT INFO
AND SUBMISSION GUIDELINES
ON THEIR WEBSITES. SO CHECK!

STEP 4!
PREPARE TO SEND!
ONCE YOU'VE GOTTEN THE
SUBMISSION GUIDELINES AND
HAVE PREPARED YOUR WORK
IN ACCORDANCE TO THEM, YOU'LL
MAKE PHOTOCOPIES OF YOUR
WORK: DON'T SEND ORIGINALS!!!
PHOTOCOPIES ARE JUST FINE
WHEN SHOWING AN EDITOR
YOUR WORK...

STEP 5!
ORGANIZE YOUR SUBMISSION
IN A NEAT, ORDERLY FASHION
AND INCLUDE A COVER LETTER
WITH YOUR CONTACT INFO, SO
YOU CAN BE CONTACTED IF YOU
STRIKE ACCEPTANCE GOLD!
IT IS WISE TO INCLUDE A SELF-
ADDRESSED STAMPED ENVELOPE IN
YOUR SUBMISSION SO AN EDITOR CAN
SEND YOU A RESPONSE REGARDING YOUR
WORK!

STEP 6!
SEND THAT BAD BOY OUT
AND WAIT ANXIOUSLY FOR
A RESPONSE...IN THAT TIME,
BUILD THE SKILLS!

# HOW TO DRAW MANGA

## STEP 1:
FIND THE CON...GO TO THE CON!
THERE ARE MANY COMIC BOOK CONVENTIONS ACROSS THE
U.S. AND CANADA EVERY YEAR. FIND THE ONE YOU WANT TO
HIT UP AND GO FORTH, GRASSHOPPER! FOCUS YOUR EFFORTS
ON YOUR STRONG POINTS, TALENTWISE, AND...

## REFINE THAT PORTFOLIO!
ONCE YOU'RE DONE FIGURING OUT WHAT IT IS YOU WANT
TO FOCUS ON, START A PORTFOLIO! A PORTFOLIO IS A
SAMPLE OF YOUR WORK THAT SHOWCASES YOUR TALENT
TO THE PEOPLE THAT MAY POTENTIALLY GIVE YOU WORK,
SO MAKE SURE YOU INCLUDE ONLY THE WORK THAT YOU
FEEL IS THE BEST REPRESENTATION OF YOUR TALENT. IT
IS ALSO A GOOD IDEA TO INCLUDE ANY PROFESSIONALLY
PUBLISHED WORK IN YOUR PORTFOLIO; THIS SHOWS THAT
YOU ARE FAMILIAR WITH WORKING WITH A PUBLISHER AND
THAT YOU HAVE WORKED PROFESSIONALLY.
THINGS TO KNOW ABOUT ASSEMBLING YOUR PORTFOLIO:
1.USE ONLY YOUR BEST PIECES.

## HITTING THE CONS

2.IF YOU HAVE A LARGE VARIETY OF WORK, MAKE SURE YOU ORGANIZE IT BASED UPON A CERTAIN THEME, SUCH AS KEEPING ALL YOUR SEQUENTIAL COMIC BOOK PAGE SAMPLES TOGETHER.

3.INCLUDE PUBLISHED SAMPLES OF YOUR WORK, IF ANY.

4.PRESENT YOUR PORTFOLIO IN A CLEAN AND ORGANIZE MANNER; DON'T CARRY AROUND A STACK OF BENT, TORN UP PICTURES. BE NEAT. AND SHOW 'EM THAT YOU'RE A PROFESSIONAL!

PORTFOLIO REVIEW
YOUR WAIT HERE WILL BE
△ [2] DAYS

WHO TO SHOW YOUR WORK TO;
MANY COMIC BOOK PUBLISHERS WHO ATTEND CONS USUALLY HAVE DESIGNATED TIMES WHEN THEY CHECK OUT PORTFOLIOS! CHECK YOUR CONVENTION SCHEDULE FOR THE TIME AND PLACE... BUT BE READY TO WAIT, FOR YOU PROBABLY WON'T BE THE ONLY ONE TRYING TO SHOW OFF YOUR WARES!

## HITTING THE CONS

TARGET PORTFOLIO REVIEWERS!
ONCE THE LINE DWINDLES AND THE SMOKE CLEARS, YOU'LL
HAVE THE EDITORS/PORTFOLIO REVIEWERS IN YOUR SIGHTS!

## HITTING THE CONS

JUST LIKE YOUR PORTFOLIO, YOU ALSO SHOULD HAVE A NEAT, CLEAN, ORGANIZED APPEARANCE. I DON'T RECOMMEND THAT YOU PLAY VOLLEY-BALL ON THE BEACH MINUTES BEFORE YOU WANT TO SHOW OFF YOUR TALENTS TO AN EDITOR. DRESS NICE AND LOOK PRESENTABLE...I'M NOT SAYING YOU HAVE TO DECK OUT IN A "VERSACE" SUIT, BUT DON'T WEAR A SHIRT WITH LAST NIGHT'S SPAGHETTI DINNER ON IT!

# HOW TO DRAW MANGA

## HITTING THE CONS

**AT LAST!**
YOU'VE REACHED YOUR "PURPOSE OPERANDI":
THE PORTFOLIO REVIEWER!
INTRODUCE YOURSELF AND BE
POLITE. NOW SHOW HIM/HER YOUR
PORTFOLIO. DON'T "DOWN" YOUR
WORK AS THE REVIEWER GOES
THROUGH IT! CREATORS TEND TO
BE THEIR OWN WORST CRITICS. SO
DON'T TALK NEGATIVE ABOUT HOW
MUCH BETTER PIECES OF YOUR
WORK SHOULD HAVE BEEN, ETC.
LET THE REVIEWER ASK THE
QUESTIONS AND YOU STAY
UPBEAT AND POSITIVE!

**343**

# HOW TO DRAW MANGA

## HITTING THE CONS

### CRITICISM!

CRITICISM OF ONE'S WORK IS HARD FOR SOME PEOPLE TO TAKE. IF A REVIEWER HAS SOME CRITICISM ABOUT YOUR WORK, THEY'RE TELLING YOU SO THAT YOU CAN IMPROVE AND GROW AS AN ARTIST. THEY'RE NOT TRYING TO PICK ON YOU OR HUMILIATE YOU. THEY'RE BASICALLY POINTING OUT WHERE YOUR WEAK POINTS ARE. SO CONCENTRATE ON THE POSITIVE POINTS AND IMPROVE UPON YOUR WEAK POINTS!